darby

Jonathon Scott Fuqua has written numerous stories, plays and articles and is an established artist, with a published collection of illustrations entitled *American Rowhouse Classic Design*. His debut novel, *The Reappearance of Sam Webber,* has received widespread acclaim in the US, winning numerous honours, including a prestigious Alex Award. The characters in *Darby* are based on a series of oral history interviews that Jonathon conducted in Marlboro County, South Carolina, over a three-year period. "I also constantly referenced the spontaneous and brilliant observations of my daughter, who sees cruelty and kindness with absolute clarity," he says. "In the end, I hope that the book does justice to good people born in troubling times, some of whom, in small ways, helped lay the foundations for change and justice." Jonathon Scott Fuqua teaches writing and art in Baltimore, Maryland, where he lives with his wife and daughter.

Also by Jonathon Scott Fuqua

The Reappearance of Sam Webber

darby

jonathon scott fuqua

WALKER BOOKS
AND SUBSIDIARIES
LONDON • BOSTON • SYDNEY

This is a work of fiction. Names, characters, places
and incidents are either the product of the author's
imagination or, if real, are used fictitiously.

First published in Great Britain 2003 by Walker Books Ltd
87 Vauxhall Walk, London SE11 5HJ

2 4 6 8 10 9 7 5 3 1

Text © 2002 Jonathon Scott Fuqua

The right of Jonathon Scott Fuqua to be identified as author
of this work has been asserted by him in accordance with
the Copyright, Designs and Patents Act 1988

This book has been typeset in Horley and Opti Typewriter Special

Printed in Great Britain by J.H. Haynes & Co. Ltd

British Library Cataloguing in Publication Data:
a catalogue record for this book
is available from the British Library

ISBN 0-7445-9056-6

For Calla, her cousins, and friends

Toads Are Safe

When I look across the cotton fields of my family's farm, the flat ground seems to rush away from my feet till it rubs the sky. From my back porch, I can see where my best friend lives. Evette's tenant house sits on my daddy's property. Together, we play out in the fields and woods, but on account of her being black and me being white, she hardly ever comes in my house, and I don't go in hers. My daddy says that's just the way it is.

Everyone around here knows my daddy because he owns a farm and the Carmichael Dry Goods store in Bennettsville, where he stocks all sorts of stuff except for the best dresses. Me and my other best friend, Beth, sometimes go visit his store after school. We sit on the counter and watch people when they come in. We like to take his elevator up and down, because you don't have to do anything but look at my daddy's helper, Russell, pulling on the ropes to make you rise. As a matter of fact, it's the first elevator in all of Marlboro County, so I suppose a lot of people come to town just so they can ride it.

When I don't go with Beth after school, my twelve-year-old brother, McCall, who, like a lot of farm kids, has been driving since he was ten, carries me home in our Chevrolet. Our farm is three miles away, so I ride with Daddy or McCall, or I got to walk. The thing is, on account of me being a girl, McCall says, "Darby, you need to sit in back till my friends are gone."

I don't like to, but I do it. One by one, his friends leap off the car without us even stopping. They sail from the hood and the running boards, and it's like watching birds fly away. I told McCall that once, and he said I was as crazy as a polecat, so I told him that girls should sit in the front seat of cars because we're better. He didn't listen, though. Instead, he socked me in my arm.

If I come straight home from school, I usually get something to eat from Annie Jane, who cooks our meals. Then I go to find Evette. Behind my house, I weave through my daddy's favorite flower bushes, his camellias, and past the pecan grove and the dairy and into the cotton fields, where the straight rows lead to Evette's door. Instead of knocking, I stand in the field and yell for her like she does when she visits me.

If she's not there, I usually feel lonely. More than anyone, she's the best person to do stuff with on our farm. Sometimes, though, she has to go off with her mama to pick cotton or boll weevils, or sometimes she just stays and plays with her friends from the black school she goes to, which makes me wish I'd stayed in town with Beth, whose brother has a pet goat and a nice riding cart that he hitches to him. Most every day that goat, Mercury, pulls Beth's brother up and down Main Street, and if I ask, he always gives me a ride.

If Evette isn't home, I usually go back through the wide fields and into my yard, where I sometimes set up a penny peek, which is a hole in the ground where you arrange pretty flowers and rocks and branches, like a window display. Other times, I go and pole-vault with an old rake handle or maybe watch Annie Jane make something that she'll let me taste. My mama says there's all sorts of entertainment on our farm, and I know it's true. I just wish Evette was around all the time instead of only a lot.

Even though the black school Evette goes to isn't as good as the Murchison School I attend in town, she's near about the smartest person I know. Mama says she gets worn-out books and poor supplies, like old maps and crumbly chalk and that sort of thing. But that doesn't seem to affect her one bit. Evette's got a brain like flypaper. Once things get stuck to it, they don't come unstuck.

Because I like her so much, last fall I did what I sometimes do. I snuck down to the basement and swiped some of my dress-up clothes, then ran across the field as fast as I could so that Mama wouldn't spot me with my hands full. When I got near Evette's house, she rushed out, and we shot off into the woods, where we played the fanciest ladies you've ever seen. She got to wear the biggest, brightest dress on account of us taking turns with it, and it was so funny, because in a real lady-like voice she stepped from around a tree, and said, "I think I wanna get a diamond so big my arm won't lift up."

"Me, too," I told her.

"I'm gonna get a wide floppy hat, too," she declared, "with flowers on it."

"I'm gonna do the same." I walked around as dainty as I could.

"I'm gonna get the longest, fanciest car and a real polite driver who only calls me *ma'am*."

I laughed at her. "Evette, blacks can't own cars."

Frowning, she said, "Girl, who told you that?"

I answered, "I just never saw it, is all."

"My aunt in New York City owns a car. She sent us a letter with a picture of it."

I stopped and gave her a look. "Are you telling the truth?" I asked.

"Yeah, I am. Also, she and my uncle Wilson own a house that's in a real nice black neighborhood. It's got four bedrooms and a library."

That being just about the most amazing thing I'd ever heard, I thought about it all afternoon. When we'd been playing for a while, I asked, "Do your aunt and uncle have electricity in their house?"

"And plumbing and gas."

Shaking my head, I said, "I just never heard of that."

"It's 'cause it's mostly a secret that blacks can be that way. But when I get older, I'm gonna write about that stuff for a newspaper. That's what my aunt does. And, when you write for a newspaper, you gotta tell the truth, and I'm gonna be famous for it. I'm gonna tell people things they wouldn't ever know."

"Like what?" I asked.

She shrugged. "I just have to think to remember things."

"You know what McCall told me that I didn't know? He said that holding a toad doesn't really give you warts."

"It's true. My big sister carried one to school, and she didn't ever get any."

"Are you gonna write about that?"

"Darby, you oughta do it your ownself. It's kinda fun, you know. You just start by saying real things, then you try and say real things most people don't know. It's like a puzzle."

I explained, "I can't do it, 'cause I don't spell so good."

"Doesn't matter," Evette answered. "That's why newspapers have editors. They check to make sure stuff is spelled right."

"Well," I said, "I don't like writing so much, either." Finding some long white gloves in the dress-up pile, I pulled them on up my arms like a movie star. "Editors are people who check spelling?"

"They do other things, too. But the checking spelling stuff is the most important."

"Mrs. Evette," I played, "it's so good to see you. Can you tell me how you know so much?"

"Well, Mrs. Darby," Evette joked back, "it's good to see you, too. And it's 'cause I ask, is how."

So that's why I began thinking I might try writing something someday, because Evette made it sound good. Still, mostly I wanted to be a mama and own the prettiest dresses and jewels and show my children how to do that trick where it looks like a person is taking her finger off at the tip.

✳   ✳   ✳

We eat dinner at six-thirty. Mama rings a bell, and if I'm a second late or wear my hat to the table, she looks at me stern. For some reason, McCall's usually late, and she always gives him the kind of unhappy eyes I can't stand. My father sits at the top of the table, next to the main dish, and me and Mama and Aunt Greer are scattered around the sides. If McCall saunters in after we've commenced to eating, my daddy shakes his head and tells him he can't go out and play the next day.

"Yes, sir," McCall always says.

The night of the day that Evette and I played dress-up in the woods, I went to my room after dinner and made a notebook for reporting, which was kind of fun, sewing it all together and making sure the pages were straight. When I had finished, I carried it down to the parlor and asked my mama, who was also sewing, if she knew about toads not causing warts.

"Darby, dear, that's just an old wives' tale."

I wrote down her comment. "Well, everyone at

school thinks it's true," I told her. "Maybe I should write an article about it?"

"Maybe you should."

"Maybe I'll write it for a newspaper?"

"Darby, dear, reporting is a man's job."

"It shouldn't be," I answered. But I could tell she didn't like me talking that way, so I tried changing the subject. "Mama, you wanna know something I learned today? I learned Evette's aunt and uncle in New York own a car and a house."

Mama laughed. "Don't believe everything that girl tells you, Darby."

"But she said she's got a picture to prove it."

"Really? You should ask her to see it, then."

"But I believe Evette, so I don't have to." Who knows what Mama thought about me saying that. I was scared to look at her.

✳   ✳   ✳

In 1878, back when cotton growing earned money, my granddaddy built our house and named it Ellan after the town in Scotland that his granddaddy came from. It's a big house, with three floors and wide hallways and pretty windows. It's painted white and has long steps that climb up to the front door and porch, where Mama sometimes sits, hiding from the sun in a rocking chair. Chimneys run all through the insides of Ellan, and we got electricity and plumbing that Daddy bought in 1916, the year before I was born. The floor is dark, and on the walls somebody painted a fake wood grain that I love because I sometimes check to see if it's real, but it never is.

From the road, our house looks like a mansion, with its whiteness and windows and porches that come off the second and third floors. You can't see the peeling paint and chipping wood at all. Rising up around the house, giant trees look like flagpoles before their limbs open halfway to the top. And on account of my daddy collecting camellia bushes, in the fall and winter we always got bright flowers around. When he's not home, I sometimes break one off and put it in my hair. Then I go hide so Mama won't see me.

In back, we got about twenty little half-tumbling-down outbuildings for holding things, including one where me and Beth wrote THE DARBY AND BETH SKOOL. When my mama saw it, though, she said that the teachers don't know how to spell, so me and Beth crossed out SKOOL and wrote SCHOOL, which looked better anyway. Later, off in the woods, me and Evette put a sign on a tree that said, THE EVETTE AND DARBY SCHOOL.

When I wrote my newspaper story on toads, I sat in the Darby and Beth School and thought for a few hours before I even started anything. It wasn't nearly as fun as Evette made it sound, either. In a way, it was like work. Frustrated, I finally started my article by saying that toads are different from frogs because they're uglier and got shorter legs. And both those things are true. Following that, I said that my mama called the wart story an old wives' tale. Then I said that McCall reads all the time, and he wants to be a doctor, and he found out that toads don't give warts, either. Last, I wrote how a girl I knew had carried a toad all day, and she never got a single wart, "and that's the truth," I put at the end.

Since McCall had been late for dinner the night before, he was home, so I carried my newspaper story up to his room for him to see.

Sitting on his bed, he read my article and looked right at me. "Darby," he said, "this isn't so good."

"Why?"

"Mostly because you only got one paragraph. You need to break it up different. You gotta have an introduction and middle part and end, and you gotta spell things right." Scratching notes beside my sentences, he said, "See?"

"Yeah," I said, hating writing.

"Aside from that, it's okay."

"You think?" I asked, perking up.

"Sure. A lotta people don't know about toads."

After dinner, I fixed my story. Then I took it to Daddy, who was sitting downstairs and drinking a glass of headache medicine. "You think this is a good newspaper article?" I asked him.

Holding my notebook, he read what I'd written. "It's very good," he told me.

"You think if I ask, Mr. Salter will put it in the *Bennettsville Times*, since you know him?"

"You'll have to check with him, honey," he said, squeezing one of my shoulders.

✳   ✳   ✳

Before Mama wakes me in the morning, somebody starts the fire in my bedroom. I stand beside it when I put my clothes on, but no matter how cold I get I try to be quiet. My aunt Greer shares my room, and I don't wanna make her stir.

Mama, McCall, Daddy, and me sit at the big table for breakfast. After saying grace, Daddy passes the grits and sausages and eggs that Annie Jane makes. When my daddy's done, he goes out and gives instructions to his farm hands. Then he drives to Carmichael Dry

Goods in the Buick. Not too much later, me and McCall leave for school in the old Chevrolet.

The morning after I wrote my story, I took it to school with me so that during lunch I could show it to Mr. Salter, who owns one of the two newspapers in town. Sitting in arithmetic, my mind wandered on to Evette, and I wondered what she would think when I showed her how fast I had become a writer. I thought for sure she'd be real proud of me.

At lunch, I straightened my dress and spit on my hands to wipe the dust off my shoes. Then I ran through the yard, over a few blocks, and up the steps to the newspaper office, where Mr. Salter and another man sat at two desks, working.

"Well, hello, Darby," Mr. Salter said.

"Hello, sir," I answered, and the walls of the news-paper office seemed about forty feet high, near about as tall as a Georgia pine.

"Can I help you?"

I nodded.

"Your daddy need something?"

"No, sir, Mr. Salter."

He stared at me. "Okay, Darby, do you need some-thing?"

"Nothing real big," I said, "except for I wrote a newspaper article, and I wanted to know whether you might put it in your paper."

"Well, Darby, what's it on?" he said, smiling.

"Toads," I said. "About how it's not true they cause warts when you pick 'em up."

Mr. Salter stood and put a hand to his chin so that he could think on what I'd just told him. He asked, "What got you to write an article?"

"On account of my friend saying it's fun."

He went over to the window behind him, then came back. "I'd have to see it before I say yes or no. Can you drop it by here later?"

My heart nearly stopped cold. "I don't need to 'cause I got it with me, sir." I gave it to him.

Opening my newspaper notebook, Mr. Salter read it slow, and I was sure he was relieved to know about toads; he smiled the whole way. "Darby, would you let me edit it a little?"

"You mean fix the spelling, Mr. Salter?"

"Mostly, yes. You can come back by and pick up your notebook after school. I'll have it copied by then."

I nearly jumped for joy. "Sure," I said. Then, with my skinny knees nearly knocking like a woodpecker on a tree, I asked, "You think I can do some more articles?"

"If you write 'em, I'll look 'em over."

Smiling, I believed he meant that I could.

Hearing Things
I Normally Don't

When I got home that afternoon, I was so happy that I skipped one of Annie Jane's snacks and rushed off through my daddy's camellia shrubs and into the cotton rows. For almost an hour, I waited for Evette. Standing close by her house, I hollered for her until I knew she wasn't home. Then I trudged back to Ellan and sat on the back steps, wanting to tell somebody about getting my story in the paper. Fidgety, I got up and started kicking a ball against a fence. Then I found my pole-vaulting stick and aimed at the hurdle my daddy had rigged for me.

I ran at the hurdle, jabbing my stick into the ground and swinging into the air and over the low bar, the same way I always do. On the other side, my feet dug into the bed of soft sand, and I was suddenly full up with so much happiness that I decided to go again. And while I was backing up, I thought that Evette was right, that it was nice to be a newspaper girl. I even thought that I might be the best and most natural one who ever lived, even better than all the boys and maybe even better than Evette, because she wasn't going to be in a newspaper any time soon. Still, one thing scared me. How was I ever going to make myself think of a good second story? It seemed like it would be real hard to find anything as easy and near as misunderstood as toads causing warts.

✳   ✳   ✳

After my daddy said grace and we started eating dinner, I said, "In case anyone wants to know, the newspaper story I was writing is gonna be in the *Bennettsville Times*. Mr. Salter told me so today."

Mama said, "Really?" She put a surprised hand against her chest.

"I never thought you'd even go ask him, Darby," my daddy said.

"One thing about you, Darby," Mama said, "you've always been stubborn."

Daddy chewed and swallowed a fork's worth of

ham. "When's the story going to run?" he asked.

"What do you mean *run*?"

"When's Mr. Salter going to put it in the paper?"

"Oh," I kind of hemmed. "Well . . . he told me he thinks it'll get *runned* next week."

Smiling, Daddy said to Mama, "I suppose he thought it was sweet."

I shook my head. "I think he just liked it."

McCall declared, "Darby, it's true. He thinks it's funny, is all."

"Does not," I replied. "He said it was real good. He . . . he told me it was one of the best newspaper reports he's ever seen." After lying, I decided to frown at McCall.

Mama clanked her fork against her water glass. "McCall, if you can't say something nice, don't say a word." She made slits of her eyes the way she did when she was a teacher at the Murchison School. Back then, she'd caused all sorts of shivers.

"That's right," my daddy told him. "Fact is, we're real proud of your sister, and the wherefore doesn't matter."

"Anyways," I went on, "Mr. Salter wants me to write more newspaper reports, too."

Dabbing the sweat on his head with a napkin, my daddy said. "Is that so? What's your next one going to be about?"

I froze.

"She doesn't even know," McCall declared.

"I do," I yipped. "Since . . . since Great-Uncle Harvey is coming for a visit, I was gonna interview him about what he does all day."

Aunt Greer said, "Darby, sweetie, he doesn't do anything but sit in his chair."

"He talks," I said, feeling a little dumb. "And he tells family stories. Anyways, I don't know for sure that I'll do him. I mean, I got other ideas."

"Yeah," McCall muttered as he ate a biscuit, "I can't wait."

Mama said, "McCall!" and she clanked her glass again.

✳   ✳   ✳

The day after Mr. Salter said he would run my newspaper article, Great-Uncle Harvey arrived for a visit. It was a Saturday, and I wanted to rush out first thing and tell Evette my news, but I couldn't, not with the way we had to clean up Ellan, especially the basement, the place where Great-Uncle Harvey usually parks himself.

At around one in the afternoon, after cleaning and

cleaning, me, Aunt Greer, Mama, and McCall loaded into the Chevrolet. Then McCall drove us all down to the train depot, where we sat and waited for the Bennettsville & Cheraw train to arrive.

Great-Uncle Harvey's real friendly and dresses good, but he can't see. When he was a kid, he lost his eyesight from the measles, so whenever he visits, he sits in a rolling chair while a black-man nurse pushes him around. As a matter of fact, when he got off the train that day we were waiting, a black-man nurse named Jacob carried him down the steps and over to us, then went back to fetch some bags and the rolling chair.

Also, since Great-Uncle Harvey is old and doesn't stand much, he isn't a good stander. So usually, when he's on his feet, he wants to hug somebody, and he was the same that day. Smiling, he said, "Now, who's here? Who's gonna give me a hug?"

My mama answered. "Great-Uncle Harvey, you got Big and Small Darby, Aunt Greer, and McCall located around you."

"Big Darby," he said, following my mama's voice and giving her a squeeze. Then he chased Aunt Greer, me, and McCall the same sort of way, following our voices.

"How are you, Great-Uncle Harvey?" Mama asked when he was done.

"I'm fine now. But that journey from Charleston is a rough, lonely ride."

Riding back to Ellan, Great-Uncle Harvey sat in the front passenger seat, discussing the smells and sounds of his trip, the way a fly had landed over and over on his cheek during the first couple of hours out of Charleston. I was stuffed in back next to my mama and Aunt Greer. Meanwhile, McCall was driving and real quiet on account of being a little mad. He had to drop us off, then go back and fetch Jacob, the black-man nurse, and he didn't want to.

"Excuse me, Great-Uncle Harvey," I said when he finally stopped talking, "you wanna go to McPherson's Pond later?" It was something me and him always did together.

"He needs to rest," Mama declared, nudging me softly with her elbow.

"That's not so," Great-Uncle Harvey told her. "A little headache medicine, and an hour of sitting, and I'm gonna want some fresh air."

"Great-Uncle Harvey," my mama said, "you've got all weekend."

"I don't mind."

Mama gave me an uncomfortable hawk-eye. "If you're gonna take him to the pond, Darby, you have to bring Jacob along with you. Either that, or you can't go."

I nodded, but I already figured Jacob was coming. I knew I wasn't strong enough to steer the rolling chair very good, and I didn't want Great-Uncle Harvey coasting out of my grip and into the water or something.

✳   ✳   ✳

The reason me and Great-Uncle Harvey always go to McPherson's Pond is so that he can get me to hear things I normally don't. He's got real sensitive ears, and he recognizes bugs and birds and bullfrogs from their noise. While we were walking, he said to me, "Darby, is there a water bird of some sort fishing the pond over yonder?" With a shaky hand, he pointed off through some sphagnum moss that was dangling in a bristle of tree limbs.

Sure enough, a bird was strolling the opposite shore, grabbing fish with a pointy beak. "How'd you know?" I asked him.

"Heard his legs stir the water."

I watched the bird for a while. Then I got curious, and asked, "Great-Uncle Harvey, do you remember what seeing was like?"

He raised a hand for Jacob to stop pushing. "Oh,

yeah," he said. "I sometimes have dreams about seeing things."

I stepped back and looked at him. "What mostly do you see in your dreams?"

"I ain't sure if I can explain it."

I brushed some burrs off my white dress. "Could you try maybe?"

Great-Uncle Harvey smiled. "I see my daddy's hands sometimes, the way they had deep cracks along the tops."

"You mean wrinkles?"

"I don't think. Cracks is what I remember, like the way the bark on a tree feels . . . except smaller."

I watched the big fishing bird lift its legs and swing into the air above the pond. So as not to make my uncle sad, I decided not to tell him that people never have cracks on their hands' tops. "Well . . ." I mumbled, "I didn't know Granddaddy except for when he was stuck in bed."

"Yeah," Great-Uncle Harvey said. "It's just something I see sometimes."

Unsure what I should say, I picked up a twig and pushed at a spider web. "Did anyone tell you I wrote a newspaper article?"

"Nobody did," Great-Uncle Harvey said. "What did you write about?"

"Just something true," I answered. "It was boring while I was doing it, but now that it's gonna be in one of the papers, I like it all right."

"Sounds good," he said.

"I just tried to tell the truth. That's what my friend says newspaper writers do."

"The decent ones," he agreed.

"That's the kind I'm gonna be," I said. I looked at the furry tops of Great-Uncle Harvey's wrists, which hung over the wooden armrests of his rolling chair. Seeing them reminded me that I'd lied about my granddaddy's hands. "Great-Uncle Harvey?"

"Yes, child?"

"Maybe I gotta say something uncomfortable."

"Well, go on and say."

I thought about how to make it sound right. "To be honest, I . . . I don't think your daddy had hands that could've been cracked that way? I never saw somebody with hands like that."

"Maybe my dreams are wrong?"

"Maybe they aren't," I said. "I just haven't ever seen it."

With a hooked finger, he loosened the collar of his nice shirt. "Fact is, it's been a long time since I saw anything."

"Great-Uncle Harvey," I whispered, "I didn't want

to tell you, but I thought I should."

"I appreciate the truth, Darby."

"That's what newspaper girls gotta do," I explained.

"It's your job," he agreed, grinning again. Then, as if he wasn't blind at all, he reached over and squeezed one of my elbows.

"How'd you know where my arm was?" I asked.

"Just did. Now go on and let's keep walking," he said, waving a hand to get Jacob to push some more.

✳   ✳   ✳

That night, after I was excused from dinner, I went downstairs and out the back door to where Jacob was smoking a cigarette in the dark. For some reason, the way he was so quiet made me curious. I stood near the doorway looking at him. Leaning against a tree, he was nearly invisible.

I said, "See that house way in the field? That's where one of my best friends lives. Her name's Evette, and she told me last week I should be a newspaper writer. That's why tomorrow I'm gonna go tell her that the *Bennettsville Times* is gonna run my story. You know what? I bet she doesn't believe me, either." I stared at Jacob, but it didn't seem like he heard me. "Can you talk?" I asked.

Jacob studied me so that I got a chill. "Course I can," he grumbled, and puffed his cigarette.

"But you don't ever say anything."

He flicked the last part of his cigarette into the dirt. "What should I be saying?"

"Just stuff."

"Child, I save my breath for folks who wansa listen."

"Oh."

He laughed. "See how me and you don't have nothing to talk about? I save my breath."

I thought for a while. Then I asked, "Do you like pushing around Great-Uncle Harvey?"

"Better than pickin' cotton."

I said, "He's real nice."

"He nice, but we don't say nothing."

"That's what it seems like."

"That's what it is," he said.

I waited a minute, then told him, "My friend who lives in that house right there is black, and she's got an aunt and uncle in New York who bought a house and a car."

He shook his head. "Up in Maryland, a black man's got hisself a whole chicken farm."

"You know what? Before the other day, I never

heard of a black person owning those kind of things."

"That's right," he said. "You wouldn't."

I watched him light up another cigarette, and just as it got to burning orange, my mama started hollering for me from deep in the house. "Darby! Darby Sinclair Carmichael, it's time for bed!"

Looking up at the back of Ellan, it seemed like I could see right through the walls to where Mama was calling for me in the hallway. I said, "I gotta go."

"That's fine, miss," Jacob answered back.

✳   ✳   ✳

When I was wearing a nightgown and ready for bed, I crept downstairs to ask Great-Uncle Harvey if I could write a newspaper story on how he was blind. Slinking through the house, I found him sitting on the back porch with my daddy. Drinking glasses of headache medicine, they weren't saying but a few words here and there.

When I caused the floor to creak, Great-Uncle Harvey said, "Who's sneaking around behind me?"

"It's me," I said.

"Darby," my daddy groaned, "it's past your bedtime."

I nodded. "Yes, sir. I just wanna ask Great-Uncle Harvey a question, is all."

"What can I do for you, child?" Great-Uncle Harvey spoke in his bullfrog voice.

Feeling more skittish than a bird, I said, "You . . . you think you'd mind if I write my next newspaper report on you being blind and hearing so well and even dreaming of seeing sometimes?"

My daddy swung about. "Darby, that's disrespectful!"

But Great-Uncle Harvey shook his head. "Naw, it ain't, Sherman. Matter of fact, I'd be honored."

Frowning at me, Daddy said, "Great-Uncle Harvey, don't feel obligated."

"I don't at all, Sherman."

I climbed up the side of his rolling chair and balanced myself on one of the armrests so that I could give him a good hug. "Thanks, Great-Uncle Harvey," I told him. "It's gonna be real fun."

Hugging back, he said, "I've never been the subject of a newspaper report before."

Making Me Mad

The next morning, I had to go to Sunday school, then to church, where I listened to our long-winded preacher. Sometimes his sermon goes so slow that my head gets woozy, and I got to leave before I faint. When that happens, McCall gets annoyed and says I embarrass him. The thing is, my daddy seems happy to go outside, where we sit on the steps and talk about the trees or the grass or something like that. Every so often, he'll say, "Reverend Macy had a whole lot to discuss today." Once he told me, "I was starting to get lightheaded, too."

When I finally got back home that morning, as fast as I could I put on a play dress and some old shoes. Grabbing up my notebook, I ran for Evette's house. As

I huffed through the cotton field behind Ellan, the sun got hot against my blond hair. Covering part of it with my hands, I yelled, "Evette! Hey, Evette! I got something to tell you!"

Sticking her head through a half-torn screen, she looked out a back window. "I'm coming out."

"I don't got long," I hissed. "In just a little bit, I gotta eat Sunday supper."

"I'll be there in a second," she said, disappearing.

Waiting for her, I threw dirt clods as far as I could. They whisked into the air and disappeared among the wavy rows of cotton plants that my daddy's mules had tilled. All around, the sky was so clear and clean it seemed like the blueness was painted on a ceiling. And on account of it being Sunday, the fields in every direction were empty. Then I heard Evette's front door slam, and I hurried around toward the side of her house, where I took hold of her hand. Together, we darted off toward the woods and hid ourselves behind a fallen-over tree trunk.

"Guess what?" I said.

"What?"

"It was a good idea about being a newspaper writer. Maybe it is fun."

"Yeah," she said, "that's what I think." She smiled. "If you wanna try it, I'll help you. We could write things together."

"That's okay. I don't need to learn any more about writing." Shrugging, I added, "Do you wanna know why?"

Real slowly, she said, "Why?"

"Well, it's 'cause my very first newspaper story is being put in the *Bennettsville Times* this week. I just took it over to Mr. Salter, and he wanted it right away. Isn't that something?"

Evette leaned against the tree trunk. "You told me you was scared to write anything."

"I was . . . but I did it anyway." I smoothed the trim of my dress so that I looked neater, more like a newspaper girl. "See, when I got home after we talked about writing for newspapers, I thought about toads and how they don't really cause warts, and since you said writing was fun, I went and tried it. I asked Mama and McCall what they thought, and I even wrote about how your sister carried one all day and didn't experience a bad side effect. Then after I showed it to my daddy, I asked him if I should take it to Mr. Salter, and my daddy didn't say much . . . so I did. I did it on Friday, and Mr. Salter must not've known about the toads, 'cause he decided to put my story in this week. So now I'm already a newspaper girl, and just a few days ago I didn't even know anything about being one. It's like I was supposed to be a girl writer all along. Doesn't it seem like that?"

Evette made the ugliest face I've ever seen. "Your daddy must've gone and asked that man to put it in the newspaper, 'cause nobody can write a good article in one try. My aunt went off to college to learn how to do it."

"My daddy didn't have anything to do with me getting in the paper. Besides, maybe writing's not easy for a lot of people, but it is for me." Sashaying my head, I added, "Guess I'm just naturally skillful."

"Darby, you ain't natural at all," she said, throwing a twig at my feet.

I swiped up a handful of dirt and poured it on top of her splitting shoes. "You're just mad 'cause I'm already a newspaper girl, and that's what you wanted to be."

"I still wanna be one, and I ain't mad," Evette announced, standing.

Looking at her, I noticed that the biggest, blackest ant was zigzagging up the middle of her dress. "You got an ant on you," I told her, knowing it would scare her something awful.

Evette shrieked and swiped at the ant like it was gonna can-opener her stomach.

"If you're so smart," I snipped, "you should know that black ants don't bite."

"It don't matter, 'cause I just don't like 'em.

36

Maybe . . . maybe your daddy didn't say nothing to the newspaper man, but the only reason you're getting your story printed is on account of who you are. That's all. It don't even matter if I can write better than you, 'cause my daddy don't own the Carmichael Dry Goods, and my daddy ain't a white man who's got his own house and farm and all that."

Standing up, I tried to make her feel dumb. "Evette, you haven't even read what I wrote, so you don't know if it's any good." I swished my notebook at her. "You know what? I was gonna let you see it, but now I guess you'll have to go buy a newspaper yourself."

"I ain't gonna go buy that fool thing." Turning away, she thumped off toward her house.

I called after her, "Your whole family can't afford a newspaper, is why you won't buy one!"

Evette spun around. Pointing at me, which my mama says is just about the rudest thing you can do, she shouted, "Darby, you smell like cow poo!"

Fearful, I sniffed myself before screeching back, "I do not!"

✳   ✳   ✳

Last year, when I caught the measles, my eyes got so weak I had to lay in bed with all the curtains plastered shut and the lights off. Everyone was nervous that I was gonna go blind like Great-Uncle Harvey. I wasn't scared, though. Back then I didn't know the measles were what broke his eyes. Instead, I fretted that Evette and Beth had forgotten about me. I didn't know their mamas were keeping them away so they wouldn't get sick. The whole time my body was coated with red dots, I worried I'd dropped out from their thoughts, which made me feel worse than itching and coughing. It wasn't till I got better that I realized they still wanted to be friends.

The thing is, I never have forgotten how lonely it was in my dark bedroom. It was awful, that's for sure. Anyways, after Evette yelled that I smelled like cow poo, I began to feel the same lonely way. Scuffing toward Ellan, I wondered if we'd ever play dress-up again. Over my shoulder, her tiny shack seemed like it was floating above the dry cotton stalks, and I wondered if she was already making plans to play with somebody who wouldn't act superior. Every few steps, I stopped and stared and imagined that I could still see the dust clouds her heels had puffed into the air.

"Evette," I said, tears bubbling in my eyes, "I'm sorry I was dumb."

Walking on past the dairy barn, which is spread out and tall and jammed with mooing cows, I knew she was right about the *Bennettsville Times*. It was hard to admit, but I knew in my heart that Evette could be a more serious and expert writer than me. She was so smart, was why.

Passing beneath the high pecan trees my grand-daddy had planted when he first built Ellan, I began wondering if I was a good writer. I even worried that McCall might be right and my article was getting in the paper for being funny instead of good. I stomped a foot. Thinking that made me as mad at him as I'd been at Evette. For a little while, it even took the fun out of getting an article run in the paper.

❋   ❋   ❋

Nobody's supposed to work on Sundays, even during the cotton harvest. So whatever time of year it is, following Sunday dinner, which commences at exactly twelve o'clock in the afternoon, we either go for a long walk around the farm or we get into the car and drive off to inspect faraway property and fields my daddy owns. Taking the car is what I like, because Daddy props open the trunk with a stick, and me and McCall sit inside it and watch the long straight roads of Marl-boro County fall off behind us. Sometimes Daddy drives on and on, and me or McCall falls asleep back there. Other times we go rattling and flopping over potholey dirt roads so that we gotta hang on for fear we might get thrown clean out. Once, when I was little, the stick that holds up the trunk shook loose and the whole heavy flap came crashing down, barely missing one of McCall's legs. Scared, I screamed as hard as I could till Mama and Daddy let us free. But I still like sitting back there. It's exciting with the trunk always threatening to mash down.

On the Sunday that me and Evette yelled at each other, my daddy decided that we should drive instead of walk, because Great-Uncle Harvey isn't sturdy on his feet. So after me and Mama and Aunt Greer did the dishes, the grownups, who were still dressed in their Sunday best, took their places inside Daddy's Buick while me and McCall got in the trunk. Daddy put the trunk-stick in place, and we flew off through the countryside toward a town called Blenheim, where a man named Dr. C. R. May invented Blenheim Ginger Ale, which is supposed to cure all nature of sicknesses but only makes my stomach churn.

Where we were seated, the wind sort of wrapped around McCall and me, tugging at our clothes so that my dress and his shirt flapped like knotted-up flags. It was nice and cool back there, the only bad thing being that I was alongside McCall, who I was mad at.

"You ain't talking to me?" he asked as a dried and squished snake disappeared behind a lump in the road.

I looked daggers at him. "It's 'cause I'm thinking about how you said Mr. Salter is putting my story in the paper on account of it being funny."

Shrugging, he threw a piece of hay into the wind so that it flew up before swooping down and bouncing along the asphalt road top. "It's Sunday," he said over the loud, blowing air, "so I ain't gonna say anything that'll make you mad."

"That's 'cause it isn't so." I slanted my eyes to show how annoyed he'd gotten me.

Hanging his feet over the trunk, like we weren't supposed to do, McCall didn't say anything back.

"If you keep doing that, you might get your legs cut off," I told him.

"I can snatch 'em back."

"No you couldn't."

"Sure I could."

Irritated, I studied his face and a fiery, red scratch on his cheek that made me think of an electric bolt. "Why're you so mean, McCall?"

"Why's putting my feet out mean?"

I had to think. "'Cause . . . if your legs get clipped off, Mama and Daddy'll have to treat you extra-nice."

Laughing, he told me, "That ain't a good reason."

"I don't care," I told him. "And you know what? It isn't true about my newspaper story."

Looking real sorry, he nodded. "I think it is." He stared at me. "It's Sunday, and I ain't trying to make you mad. You know how Daddy always says getting good jobs is who you know. Well, Mr. Salter knows you, and he was probably thinking it might make people laugh a little. What's wrong with that? Making people laugh is a real good reason to do almost anything."

I sat motionless alongside McCall and could hardly speak without choking. Finally, I said, "I wish he'd taken it for how good it is."

"If it makes people laugh, that's okay. That's all right."

Sucking on the smoothness of a tooth, I dropped my head and thought about the way I'd been snobby to Evette. I wished I could run to her house and make up. I looked at my brother instead.

"McCall," I said, "why don't you have any best friends?"

Hanging a piece of straw between his lips, he answered, "I don't know. I like people well enough. I suppose I just like being with me most of all."

"Even when you're by yourself?"

"Yup."

I stared at the straight asphalt road that my daddy said hadn't been there when he was a boy. Back then, all the roads had been made of dirt. Out of nowhere, a gang of black birds dashed slantways past the trunk in a great twirling flash. Altogether, they raced away and across the wide, wide cotton fields.

"Wish I could catch me one a them," McCall declared, gawking at those birds.

✳   ✳   ✳

Whenever we're driving near Blenheim, we've always got to visit my daddy's family gravesite. After the cotton and tobacco fields come to an end, and patches of woods start up, there's this tiny cemetery without a fence, and that's where all of my daddy's kin get buried. I don't mind going there on account of my daddy telling stories about his granddaddy and how he went off to fight in the Civil War in Richmond and Antietam with General Stonewall Jackson. Daddy usually talks about how after the war his granddaddy came home and saved money for three years before starting Carmichael Dry Goods. Also, if Great-Uncle Harvey's with us, he's always got things to add. His favorites are how our family came from Scotland and how they got off the boat with nothing but determination.

"Great-Uncle Harvey," I said, leading him through the graveyard, "why do you wanna come here if you can't see anything?"

For a second, he moved his hand from my shoulder and straightened a sleeve of his fancy suit. "Sure enough, I can't see nothing. That's true. But I can feel my kin wrastling in my bones. I can feel us walking on top of 'em."

"Is that why you didn't bring your rolling chair, so you could walk?"

"Naw, child, it didn't fit into your daddy's car is why I left it with Jacob."

I nodded.

We walked about some more, and Great-Uncle Harvey said, "Little Darby, when you gonna interview me about being blind?"

"Maybe tonight, if it's okay?"

The truth was, since recognizing that my story on toads was in the paper for being funny, I didn't wanna ask him anything. I kept imagining all of Marlboro County laughing at my article, and it was embarrassing, especially standing atop all my successful and determined kin.

I stopped so that Great-Uncle Harvey would. "Here's your mama," I told him.

"Touch my hand to the gravestone," he said.

So I did, and while he smiled, I looked across the little clearing to where my daddy and Mama and Aunt Greer were crouched near another marker. Behind them, I saw McCall riding a pine tree by climbing to the top and letting it bend to the ground real slow.

*   *   *

Cold, I tucked my favorite nightgown, which Mama had sewn from our best window curtain, underneath my legs. Great-Uncle Harvey and me sat out on the screened porch, and there was a cool wind blowing, clacking the pecan trees and rustling the dried-up cotton plants in the field, which gave off a soft *shoosh* like my daddy's new radio when nothing comes in.

"Great-Uncle Harvey," I started, turning my newspaper notebook to a blank page, "what's it like to be blind?"

Great-Uncle Harvey smiled and looked near me. "What's it like to be blind? I'd say it's real dark."

Trying to act professional, I nodded my head and wrote that down. "But . . . you can hear real good, can't you, sir?"

"Like you wouldn't believe, ma'am," he kidded me. "I can smell good, too."

For a minute, I stalled on knowing what else to ask. Thinking hard, I finally said, "Is it nice to hear real well?"

Great-Uncle Harvey shrugged his wide shoulders. "It's okay. I enjoy the fact that a lot of other people don't hear as good. Matter of fact, I take great pride in pointing out things I hear to people who can see, 'cause they're always surprised. I can tell you if a bird's in a tree and, if it sings, what kind it is. I can tell you if there's a cat or a squirrel scampering in the woods . . . I can hear things like the walls and floors creaking in a house and tell you if a place is old or new —"

"Great-Uncle Harvey?"

"Yes, child?"

"I can't write that fast."

"Sorry," he said, grinning.

"My hand gets all cramped, is why."

"Can't say I ever had a hand cramp."

So there we were, and he talked slower and told me about how he could read things that were written in Braille, which is this way of spelling words with bumps. He said he could do it with his fingertips and that some books were written up that way just for blind people. He said that he liked to eat because he tasted food real well. Then he said he liked dressing nice like he did to show that blind people care about their appearance. He also decided that his favorite thing to do is to listen or tell stories, and another thing he liked was to get pushed around Charleston in his rolling chair. He said that when Jacob took him around the city that way, he heard birds and water and all sorts of people talking.

Finally, Great-Uncle Harvey paused, and asked, "So, Darby, when is this here article on me gonna be completed? You got any idea?"

"So that Mr. Salter can see it before the weekend, I'm gonna try and get it done by Friday."

"You gonna mail me a copy?"

"You think somebody'll turn it into bumps for you?"

"Naw, a nurse'll just read it to me, probably. It'll give me a chance to brag on you some."

I smiled, clamping my jaw shut so that my teeth wouldn't tap from being cold. My body had been so trembly, though, that it looked like I'd been writing while I was bouncing in my daddy's car. "I'm gonna write about you real good," I said.

"You do that," he said. "Now I'm all talked out, so you run on to bed 'fore you catch your death out here."

Staring at his face, I asked, "Great-Uncle Harvey, how'd you know I was cold?"

He answered, "On account of the way your voice sounds."

A Pure Genius

At night, sometimes, I can't sleep even with my aunt Greer nearby. It's an awful feeling. I wake up with the worst fright and listen to the owls and the crickets and a few last bullfrogs. And even though I recognize everything, their noises scare me all the way to my heart. Looking around my room, first at my aunt Greer to be sure she's the one breathing heavy, I study the walls and the windows and the shadows flittering, and the whole bunch looks ghoulish. Whenever I wake up that way, I think about that mansion in Bennettsville that was owned by Mr. Grissel, who during the Civil War was in charge of fetching boys who didn't want to fight. He fixed it so they either did fight or were shot. Of all of the haunted houses in Marlboro County, his is the most famous. He choked on a possum bone way before I was born, but nobody ever bought his property. Everyone knows that all the ghosts of the boys he caused to get shot are walking around that house looking to get even with Mr. Grissel. I suppose, for some reason, they don't even know he's dead yet. For nothing, I wouldn't step in that mansion during the day or night. The problem is, sometimes I wonder if Ellan isn't haunted the same way, because in the dark it can scare me so that I nearly have to holler for help.

Just a few hours after I talked with Great-Uncle Harvey, my mind stirred with all sorts of frightening things. Sitting up, I imagined ghosts whooshing between the tree limbs outside, floating past my daddy's camellia bushes, with shoulders that were almost see-through.

Searching about the room, I wished our dog, King, was nearby. King wouldn't be scared of a ghost, plus his teeth are sharp enough to cut through just about anything. If I'm walking alone near McPherson's Pond, I usually take King in case I run into a mean person or something rabid or an alligator. Being a German shepherd dog, King's nearly as smart as a college teacher, too. When I talk to him, his big, triangular fur ears do all sorts of shifting and adjusting, like he's listening as hard as he can. Sometimes I even practice the finger trick for him. It's the only thing he doesn't understand real well, and I'm glad. He never recognizes when I mess up and my finger doesn't look cut off.

The other good thing about King is that he walks Annie Jane home at night. After arranging and setting out our dinner, Annie Jane takes off her apron and starts out the back door, where he waits for her. Then, side by side, the two march toward town and Annie Jane's little home with its skinny rooms that go straight back so that you can run from the front door to the back without ever turning, not once. Daddy calls it a "shotgun house."

Awake in the night like I was, I wished my mama allowed King to come upstairs, but she doesn't. She says letting a dog in the house would be like letting a muskrat make himself cozy. From time to time, I feel like saying that a muskrat can't protect a person against ghosts, not like a dog with extra-pointy teeth and lots of brains.

I slid under my sheets and squeezed into a tight ball so that all a ghost might see was a bundle of blankets and bed sheets. Sucking air real slow, my heart thumped in my body, and I started to get as hot as a wagon in the sun. Lying that way, so still and warm, I didn't have anything to do but wonder why I was nervous. I thought and thought. Then, as slow as a snail, I realized that it had to do with Evette, and understanding that made things less scary. On account of being nasty to her, I was feeling crummy. It wasn't that I was frightened. Guilt had woken me up. It was like the time I'd fetched a farm hand's thrown-away cigarette and took a puff. I knew I'd been a bad person, and I wondered what God thought.

✳   ✳   ✳

The next day, as McCall drove us home from school, I sat in the back seat while his friends jumped off the car like always. I didn't say anything about how girls were better than boys or how I should sit up front. Instead I stayed quiet so I could concentrate on being ashamed.

At Ellan, I changed into a play dress and ran out back. Stumbling through the rows of cotton, I sat half-hidden and looking at Evette's front door and the tiny garden that her parents had planted full of scrappy vegetables. I sat for more than an hour, picking at cotton leaves and throwing pieces of dirt before I finally saw Evette and her younger brother start toward me down the long, unpaved road that connects their house to the highway.

As they got near, I could hear her brother, Joebean, say, "He got his ankle broke and both wrists, and his whole face and neck swelled up."

Evette answered. "He wasn't thinking. You get caught grabbing one a them chickens and you might get kilt."

After a few steps, Joebean answered, "Yeah, he almost did."

When they were close by, I stood so they could see me. "Hey, Evette."

She stared for a second before answering real softly. "Hey, Darby."

"I gotta tell you something."

"What's that?"

Swallowing, I looked at my shoes. "I . . . I was gonna say *sorry*, is all."

Jumping the wood steps to their house, Joebean passed through the rickety screen door. Evette watched it slam.

I told her, "I'm real apologetic for yesterday."

"We done it to each other," she said. "We was both mean."

"I wish we were friends again."

"Me too."

"You wanna be?" I asked, blushing.

She acted like she was thinking. "Yeah . . . that'd be

nice," she answered.

Relieved, I said, "And we can write articles together, and I'll know the reason why my story is in the newspaper. I promise."

"That's all right, Darby. You don't gotta say anything like that."

My eyes filled with tears. "You wanna go play right now?"

"I can't until after I change," said Evette.

"I'll wait. Then, if you want, we can go swing or something? You want?"

She smiled, and replied, "All right," and ran into her house to change into play clothes. And finally I stopped feeling like I had the measles and was stuck in a dark room, worrying all by myself.

✳   ✳   ✳

In late October, when you stand on Ellan's front porch, it looks like the sun crashes out of the sky and sinks into the far-off trees like a daub of butter melting on a piece of bread. It's a real strange sight, making it hard for me to think that the earth is spinning. Sometimes, I sit down and try figuring it out in my head, how the earth and the other planets are circling the sun and twirling separately all at the same time.

For once, though, as the sun sank, I didn't think about that sort of thing. Instead, I wrote my article about Great-Uncle Harvey. Writing wasn't nearly as bad as the first time, either. At least I didn't hate it. Anyways, right off I said that Great-Uncle Harvey is blind but has real good senses and can hear just about anything, even me when I'm trying to sneak up behind him. I said that he can tell birds by their voices and that his fingers can read bumps that are like a blind person's alphabet. I explained how he dresses good and how his shoulders are broad, and that he rides in a rolling chair and nearly always has since the measles made him blind. Recollecting our walk beside McPherson's Pond, I wrote that he sometimes has dreams of seeing his daddy's hands and that he can't tell if it's a memory or if he's recalling them wrong on account of the way they're so cracked along the tops. Most of all, though, I said that Great-Uncle Harvey was real nice and that he didn't let being blind make him ornery.

Closing my newspaper notebook, which had only a few more pages left, I stared at the sun melting away as the fields of my daddy's farm turned purple and the sky above became darker and darker pink. I wished I had a dress made of such good colors. I thought that I could go to every party wearing that dress and that all the boys might like me, and that all the girls would wish they owned it, but they wouldn't. It would just be mine.

Leaving off the steps, I passed into Ellan's hallway with its fake wood walls. Then I went into the kitchen, where Annie Jane was getting dinner together. "Hey, Annie Jane," I said to her.

"Whatcha doing, Darby?" Annie Jane put her fists atop her hips.

I slumped against the tabletop. "I just wrote a newspaper story."

"Well, good," she said, but I could tell she didn't care.

"I'm writing it on Great-Uncle Harvey."

"He a good story," she agreed.

Nodding, I watched her remove two loaves of bread from the oven. She held the two tins with dishrags Mama had made out of grain sacks. "Can I have a slice of that?"

"Child, no. Mr. Carmichael'd get upset. There's ten minutes till dinner. You gotta hold tight."

My stomach growled, and I shuffled away and leaned against one of Ellan's tall walls. Outside it was so dark blue it looked like fountain pen ink. "Annie Jane, you think I'm pretty?"

Tossing a towel over her shoulder, she said, "Darby,

you a beautiful little girl, that's for sure."

"You think I'd be prettier if I had a purple and pink dress?"

"You'd look purty in a paper sack, child. You don't need no lavish dress."

Atop the dirt drive, I saw lights splash, then rise up and hit trees, the smokehouse walls, and even the chicken house behind it, and I knew my daddy was back from town. A few minutes later, he creaked up the steps and into the kitchen. Spotting me, he waved the *Bennettsville Times* in the air. "Your story's inside," he told me. "I had people coming in the store all day, telling me they saw it."

Nervous, I asked, "Did they laugh?"

"They were real impressed," he promised, relieving my nervousness and distracting me so that I forgot about the dress. He showed me my article sitting at the bottom of a page. In bold letters it said, "Seems Toads Aren't So Awful." Then in small letters it said, "By Little Darby Carmichael."

I smiled. "I was just hoping to tell the truth about something."

"Well, you sure did."

My aunt Greer and Mama wandered in alongside each other.

I squealed, "Daddy's got my newspaper story!"

They came to take a look at "Seems Toads Aren't So Awful."

Jacob carried Great-Uncle Harvey up the steps and placed him at the kitchen table for dinner. Great-Uncle Harvey asked, "What's all the commotion for?" as he felt around for his napkin and water glass. I told him about my story.

"Now that's really something," he declared.

During dinner, which McCall was late for, my whole family treated me like a motion picture star, like I was Mary Pickford instead of Darby Carmichael. It was nice. I let them all say something good, and I wished they'd keep doing it. Even Annie Jane got into the act. Before leaving for home, she stopped over and declared I was *a pure genius,* which was real wonderful to hear, even though I know she can't read.

Turpin Dunn

At least three times a week, McCall drives us to school fifteen minutes early so he can get the lowdown on people. On those days, me and Beth rush to our classroom and tell each other secrets and stories about everyone we know. That's how it always goes. The thing is, the day after "Seems Toads Aren't So Awful" came out wasn't normal. I didn't care about any gossip. The first thing I wanted to know was whether Beth had read my article.

"My daddy did," she answered.

"Why didn't you?"

"'Cause I fell asleep so early I didn't get a chance."

I nodded. "So what did your daddy say?"

"He thought it was cute."

I looked at the floor. "He didn't think it was

professional-sounding?"

Beth said, "He thought it was nice and funny."

"Oh," I mumbled as my eyes watered up.

"He thought it was real smart, too. He said, 'Darby's so smart.'"

I lifted my head a little bit. I knew she was lying, but I didn't care. "Thanks."

"For what?" Beth asked. Then she made her perfect smile, which is something she has. As a matter of fact, last Christmas I asked God for her lips instead of mine. The reason is, Beth's lips are just right. They're sort of plump, and the bottom half kind of puckers while the top part has an exact triangular notch in the middle. They're beautiful, that's for sure. If she sneaks her mother's fancy shoes, she looks like a picture show star.

Our friends Helen and Sissy and Jack-Henry and Boog and Shoog came in and sat down like a pack of wild animals, causing their desks to skid and scrape on the wood floor. A few minutes later, the kids from the Mill Village, the Lint Heads, stomped up the steps and through the door. Since their daddies weave cotton in a factory, they're considered low-class. That's why me and my friends didn't say anything to them.

My school, the Murchison School, was built by a lady named Harriet Beckwith Murchison, who once taught music in Bennettsville before finding a rich man to marry and becoming rich her ownself. She had the biggest, showiest tastes, too, so our school isn't just the handsomest in Marlboro County, it's also made of the best stuff. Mama often says Mrs. Murchison was an angel for giving kids such a wonderful place to learn inside of. I suppose she's right.

The thing is, even though it's got all the newest and best, there is one fancy thing the Murchison School doesn't have. There's nowhere to sit and eat inside. I guess Mrs. Murchison figured that people could walk home for lunch, not reckoning that farm kids from way out in the county would attend. So while my friends go on to their own houses, I have to eat at this apartment building around the block. All the teachers live there, since state law says in order to teach, they can't be married and have got to be from out of town. McCall, he doesn't take to that arrangement, so he skips food and goes off to catch bugs or birds or to read a book. In a way, I'd rather do that, too. My problem is that my stomach gets starved.

The day after "Seems Toads Aren't So Awful" was in the paper, though, I didn't mind eating with the teachers and farm kids. It wasn't like usual, where I had to be mannerly and not say anything unless I was spoken at, which normally isn't too often. Every teacher at my table, all five, praised my story and me for taking such a big interest in language and writing. They didn't quit, either, so that the whole way through my meal I had to concentrate on seeming humble.

"Thank you, ma'am," I said a million times. "I just wanted to tell the truth."

"Well, you did a wonderful job," one of them promised me.

Another teacher said, "I hope you'll keep getting better."

"I'm gonna, ma'am," I answered her.

She corrected my English. "You are going to," she said.

"That's what I meant," I told her.

"Fine," she replied, and took a bite of the salty ham.

"You've raised the bar for all of your peers," my teacher, Miss Burstin, announced.

I thought about what she had said. "I hope no one gets mad at me for doing that, ma'am."

"Don't you worry about others," she instructed.

"Yes, ma'am," I said, but as soon as I thought about it, I did worry. I didn't want to make anyone look bad.

"I'm going to give you an extra-credit grade," Miss Burstin told me.

I stared at her. "What grade are you gonna give me, ma'am?"

"Why, Darby, an A, of course."

Smiling, I said, "Thank you, Miss Burstin." Then, because I was worried they'd see how their compliments were swelling my pride, I tried not to smile.

✳   ✳   ✳

Tip-tapping through the dry, skinny streets of Bennettsville, me and Beth headed to her house. Cheerful, we danced along with our elbows locked together like a chain. Even though my mama would've gotten mad, I grabbed the sides of my dress and lifted them a little so that I could kick a foot high in the air.

"How did that look?" I asked Beth.

"So beautiful," she said.

"You do it."

She shook her head. "If my mama saw me, I'd be in trouble for a week."

"That's why it's fun," I told her, and did it again.

"You look like a Broadway dancer."

"I wish I was," I said, high-kicking about.

"Not me," Beth announced. "If I could make a wish, I'd make one to live in England."

Letting go of her arm, I asked, "Why?"

"'Cause they got kings and princes and such there. In America, we won't ever get a chance to meet those sorta people. My daddy says that instead of having a monarchy like they got, we have a democracy run by normal people. We don't have kings or queens or anything."

Hearing that got me a little sad. Since the first grade, me and Beth had always wanted to be princesses and have jewels and whole rooms full of expensive clothes. "Maybe we can move to England after school?"

"Maybe we'll both find a prince?"

"I bet," I told her. Then I tried to act like I was from London. In a fancy voice, I said, "Mrs. Fairchild, what are me and you gonna play today?"

She raised up her shoulders and gave me an expensive look. "We could make penny peeks, Mrs. Carmichael."

I said, "Then maybe we can ride in Chester's royal goat cart and have Mercury pull us to my daddy's store?"

A playfulness came into Beth's face. Smiling, she said, "You know what? I'm sure Chester's gonna let you ride. He likes you, is why. My brother's got a crush and thinks you're pretty."

Stopping to stare into her eyes, I hissed, "He does

not!" Suddenly I was frightened and excited about seeing Chester.

"He does. He says you got a sweet face and you're good about helping him feed Mercury."

"I like Mercury, is all."

✳   ✳   ✳

Beth's house sits alongside the biggest, nicest homes in all of Bennettsville. That's because it's one of them. It's got a wide porch and three tall floors of rooms, and windows that always sparkle they're so clean. Sometimes I think President Coolidge ought to live there because it even has a little balcony off the second floor he could wave from. It's big, too. It can make Ellan look miniature to me. My daddy says Beth's daddy, Mr. Robert Fairchild, is Marlboro County's best lawyer, and a real good person to boot, and he says that their home has to be that good. I reckon he's right.

When we got to Beth's house, her brother was out with Mercury, and I was glad. Seeing him would've turned me as pink as a flower. Thankful, I set my books alongside Beth's on the back steps and fetched a piece of bread from the cook. After we were done eating, we went out into the yard to make our penny peeks.

Careful, we dug perfect, round holes in the ground. Then we collected flowers and rocks from Mrs. Fairchild's giant garden. Away from each other, me and Beth arranged things in our holes, both of us fixing to make a more beautiful display than the other. After a good while, we got them just the way we wanted, with every flower turned to its best side. We went into the shed and carried over sheets of glass, and, careful not to mess up our work, we laid them on top of our penny peeks so that they looked like store windows.

We stepped back.

After about a minute, Beth asked, "Which is prettier?"

Walking over to her penny peek, I looked at the leaves and the mums and camellias and slightly shriveled petunia buds. They were so nice I smiled.

She was hunched over mine. "Yours is the best."

"They're both nice."

She said, "Let's not play that somebody has to win, Darby."

"All right," I agreed.

❋   ❋   ❋

At my daddy's store, me and Beth sat on the downstairs counter, watching folks come in. We knew everyone, and nearly all of them had read "Seems Toads Aren't So Awful." Stepping through the doors, they called hello to us before telling me how impressed they were. Some said they had no idea toads were so safe, and others congratulated me by squeezing my knee or messing up my hair, which is something I don't like.

Outside, Bennettsville was full up with people buying or selling or talking about things that farmers and townsfolk discuss. The stores up yonder and down the street were busy and nice with their columns and swirly-whirly parts and windows. Workhorses stomped past pulling wagons, and a few cars clitter-clanked along with engines that sounded like metal animals. Across the street, our courthouse seemed as if it had been kidnapped clean out of Washington, D.C. Its big, important-seeming tower stood out against the baby blue sky, which is one of my favorite colors on account of its name: *baby blue.*

Alongside us, my daddy's gold cash register was ringing, but it didn't seem like people were handing over money. Instead, they signed their names to receipts and walked straight out with their ropes and harnesses and barbed wire spools or whatever. Most of them said, "Bye, Little Darby and Beth Fairchild."

"Bye, Mr. Turley" or "Mr. MacNight" or "Mr. Jones," we said back, grinning and drumming our heels against the wood counter. Sitting there, I wished so bad we could go to the Candy Kitchen for a brown cow or a chocolate. Finally, I turned and asked my daddy for a nickel.

My daddy stopped punching numbers into the register and looked at me without any kind of mood on his face. After what seemed like a hundred minutes, Mr. Walter Henry, who was standing at the register, said, "Here now, let me give ya a dime, what with how much I owes Carmichael Dry Goods."

"Don't, Walter," my daddy said to him.

"Come on, Mr. Carmichael."

"Naw, you keep your money till you can pay on your bill."

Hesitating, Mr. Walter Henry looked at the dimes and nickels in his dirty palm. Breaking into a smile, he lifted his shoulders at me and Beth, and said to my daddy, "If that's the way you want it, Sherm." Grabbing hold of a potato sack and a new shovel handle, he carried them out the door.

Next in line was Mr. Turpin Dunn, who is one of the biggest and meanest men in the whole world. He must be ten feet tall, with a chin that's as sharp and straight as a plow blade and eyes sitting on his face like two blazing drips of cooking lard. His farm touches one side of ours, and in the winter when the trees are naked, we can see his flickery oil lamps burning away in his windows. McCall and me always walk through other people's property without a care, but we don't get close to his land. Reason is, he's got a bad reputation. Tenant kids say he threw a black boy, a little boy, against a smokehouse wall for eyeing his mean old wife. The thing is, it's hard not to give her a good peek. It isn't that she's ugly or has something nasty on her, it's the way she pinches her face so hard. It's funny-seeming. Anyways, after that boy got thrown, he turned stupid and never got normal. That's what the tenant kids say.

When I see Mr. Dunn, something I always notice is how he's missing the tip of one of his pinkies. What I heard is he got it thrashed in a cotton gin when he was little. I figure that could make him act angry. As for Mrs. Dunn, I heard Mama say she looks that way on account of life with him.

My daddy said to Mr. Dunn, "Things going okay, Turpin?"

Crinkling up that sharp chin, Mr. Dunn said, "All right, I guess. It never is easy or simple, though, is it?"

"Only on Sundays," my daddy declared, laughing. But I knew they didn't much like each other. Mr. Dunn believes that our dog, King, walks all of a round-trip mile to poop in his front yard.

Mr. Dunn said, "Sundays might be simple for you, but they don't seem so simple to me, Sherman. They ain't what they used to be, that's for sure. Matter of fact, just two nights ago, that would be a Sunday, I caught me a black boy stealing chickens outa my hen house. I say to him, 'You gotta tell me you're sorry for doing this.' But he don't. Boy didn't apologize and wouldn't give me his name or nothing. I didn't recognize him, and I'm sure he ain't one a mine 'cause they wouldn't be that stupid." He looked at my daddy hard.

My daddy looked at him back.

"Anyways," Mr. Dunn started up again, "I don't gotta tell you that even on a Sunday, it made me furious. I liked to feel crazy with the lack of respect he shown me and all I give to blacks in the fields. They already got too much and they stealing mine."

"That's a shame," Daddy offered.

Mr. Dunn scratched a patch of beard stubble. Then he said, "Sherm, they act like we owes 'em, and I don't cotton to that kinda behavior, not for ten seconds. You know me. I'm a fair, honest man, but I don't like it. You take a look at that Ossian Sweet character up in Detroit last year. Had the nerve to move into a white neighborhood. Then he acts surprised people wanna drive him out. Don't that beat all?" Mr. Dunn bent down so that he could point right at my daddy. "Now, that boy I caught, he won't be doing nothing like stealing chickens for a good while. You don't gotta worry about him coming around your place."

Daddy said, "I see."

Mr. Dunn signed a receipt and straightened and glanced at me with those burning-lard eyes of his. "Eh, now, Darby, thanks to you, I ain't gonna worry 'bout toads no more."

"I'm real glad, Mr. Dunn," I said softly.

"Bye-bye, Beth Fairchild," he said, stepping away, tools in his hand.

"Bye, Mr. Dunn," she answered.

When he was gone, I had the willies so bad that I didn't want to sit anymore. "Beth," I said, "you . . . you wanna go ride the elevator or something?"

"Yeah!" she answered, and we leaped off that old counter.

"Hey, now, you girls are gonna wear Russell out," my daddy called to me.

"We won't," I promised. "Besides, he likes pulling the ropes," I said. But I could tell that Russell really didn't. After a whole day of hauling heavy things between the first and second floor, he must feel like somebody's nearly yanked his arms off.

On the way home, my daddy was quiet. "Darby?" he finally said.

"Yeah, Daddy?"

"You embarrassed me today, asking for money in front of all those men."

Surprised, I sat quiet for a few minutes. "Sorry, Daddy" was what I said back. And I really was sorry. I felt like a bad person for embarrassing him.

"You didn't know," he told me, "but these days, after everyone's paid off their bills from the tobacco and cotton harvest, they start working on the next bill, and we don't take in much cash. So, to put it real simple, we don't really have money to waste."

"Okay," I answered.

We rumbled through town, past big and small homes. There was a patch of forest before we passed by Annie Jane's neighborhood. Another patch of forest came after that. Then we were on the open highway, the cotton rows swaying like tiny ballerinas. When we got closer to Ellan, my daddy said, "Can you believe that Turpin Dunn? He actually came in and accused one of my tenant farmers' boys of trying to steal his chickens. That man doesn't know when to quit."

Shocked, I said, "He was doing that?"

"Yeah, and it wasn't real subtle, either."

"Daddy, what's *subtle* mean?"

"It means, he didn't do it in a smart way. It means he just threw it out there like he didn't care if it made me mad."

Something in the Night

In late October, if it doesn't rain, the afternoons are so bright you've got to squint. After school gets out, it's the worst. Sunbeams get as long and sharp as pins. Also, daylight goes away so fast you've got to go inside early, even if you're having fun.

What's happy about late October is that my birthday is on Halloween. My mama and daddy always plan something fun for the weekend closest to my birthday, and they invite all my friends from school. They've got one rule, though: They don't want me discussing my party or presents ahead of time. So even if it's a week away, it can seem a lot further.

Overnight, the weather had turned cold, so, going downstairs for breakfast, I bunched myself in a thick sweater. Scooting past the fake wood paneling in our hallway, I touched it to make sure it hadn't turned real. Going into the kitchen, I saw Mama and Great-Uncle Harvey at the table, already eating bacon and biscuits with eggs. I was about to slip onto a chair when my eyes noticed something out the back window. Our wash house was billowing steam like the Bennettsville & Cheraw Railroad. Warm clouds flew out of the open door, and I could imagine all my dirty dresses bubbling clean in that big iron cauldron of boiling water that was full up with soap.

"Good morning, Darby," Great-Uncle Harvey called.

I sat down and said, "Good morning."

Mama asked, "Did you sleep well?"

"Yes, ma'am," I answered. Then, staring at Great-Uncle Harvey, I asked him, "How'd you know it was me?"

"It's the way you walk, dear."

As keen as his ears work, they aren't any bigger than normal. That always surprises me a little. "It's like you're part magic."

"Sorta," he agreed.

I told him, "I wish you weren't gonna leave today."

Mama said, "We're all sorry he's going."

Smiling, Great-Uncle Harvey said, "Course, it's

75

been a fine trip. I won't deny that, but now I need to return to my routine. If I don't, I might get spoiled and not ever leave."

"I'm gonna send you my article."

"That's what I expect."

McCall thumped down the steps. Banging into the kitchen, he dumped himself into a chair, and said, "Sorry."

"You're excused," Mama told him.

✳   ✳   ✳

On the third day after my article was out, everyone forgot about it. At school, I was treated like the same regular girl as before. Even at lunch my teachers didn't praise me. Arriving home, I grabbed what I'd written about Great-Uncle Harvey and carried my newspaper notebook out back. On the fence beside the dairy barn, I sat snuggling in my coat and watching for Evette. Behind me, I could hear cows scraping against wood pens.

When I finally saw Evette and her two brothers kicking up a dust cloud, I ran through the field and yelled for her. Not ten minutes later, me and her chased off and sat in the woods beneath a tall tree with limbs stretching wide and as round as a ball. It was there that I showed her my story on Great-Uncle Harvey.

"It needs some changing." Steam flittered about her mouth before disappearing.

"Why?" I asked, worried that she was still jealous and trying to make me scared about newspaper work.

"'Cause, Darby, see here how it ain't so smooth?" Evette flipped to a page of my story and read me some.

"So what?" I said, rubbing my hands together to keep them warm.

"My aunt says you gotta finish one idea 'fore you jump into the next. See, the way your uncle can read bumps don't got one thing to do with the way he listens to birds. Understand?"

I did, but it was hard to admit. "I guess." Feeling kind of dumb, I said, "Maybe . . . maybe you could help me with it? I wanna make it good on account of how nice Great-Uncle Harvey is."

Evette smiled her pretty smile, which is sort of like Beth's except her lips are darker. She said, "Oh, you can make it good. You can make it real strong, 'cause it ain't half-bad. It'll be as easy as pie, almost." Then me and her got working and didn't finish until the sun started melting like butter, and I got confused again about how the earth circles and spins through space.

Walking back to her house, Evette shivered, and told me, "Think like this: The earth spins all by its ownself. It's like one a them tops. While it's doing that, it's also makin' a wide circle round the sun. You got that?"

"No," I said, feeling dense.

"It don't matter."

Near her house, I said, "You think my article's okay?"

"It's real good," she answered, flittering around playful-like with her long, patchy coat. I looked down and saw that above her falling-apart shoes, her socks were wide open and fraying at the tops.

"Evette?" I said.

"Yeah?"

"How come you can write so good, but you don't talk right?"

She shrugged. "Guess 'cause I talk like my mama and daddy and brothers, but I writes like my teachers."

I nodded. "Thanks for helping me."

"I like doing editing," she said. Turning, she ran down a narrow row and into her little yard. Walking up the bouncy, creaky steps, she spun and waved. Waving back, I felt glad she was my friend. Then she yanked back her ripped screen door and passed through the big door behind it.

78

That night I woke up scared again, or I thought I did. Searching around for a ghost, I saw Aunt Greer sitting up in her bed, breathing clouds of steam into the cold air. That's how I knew something was happening. "What's going on?" I asked.

Aunt Greer didn't answer. One thing about her is that she doesn't like to be surprised or frightened. She gets tearful from it. That's the reason she sleeps in my room. She says that she has to be close by a person or her heart feels like it's about to burst.

Outside, King was barking and I heard faint voices. Curious, I got up from my bed and was about to head out the door when Aunt Greer hissed at me. "Darby! You can't leave."

I hung on my toes. "Come on with me, Aunt Greer," I whispered.

"I can't," she said worriedly. "You gotta stay."

On account of her, I was stuck, so I rushed into the bathroom, where I stood on the water closet's seat and cracked the window.

Right away, I heard my daddy talking. He said, ". . . and some aspirin, some compresses, and a disinfectant of some sort."

"What kind of disinfectant?" Mama asked.

"Rubbing alcohol or moonshine. Just something!"

Mama answered, "Okay," and I could hear her race

through the downstairs.

My daddy asked someone, "Where's the boy?"

A black man answered, "He at my house, sir."

"Which is where?"

Another black man said, "Mr. Carmichael, it's up the roads a short ways."

"We're gonna take my car over," Daddy said.

"But . . . but, sir, oh, Lawd, that boy, he needs hisself a doctor bad."

"Then we'll take him to Bennettsville."

The black man sounded worried. "Who gonna see a black boy at this time a night? Who gonna?"

"Dr. McNeil," my daddy answered.

When Mama came back, Daddy and the two black men raced through the darkness for the car barn. A moment later, the Buick was cranked and clacking wildly from the coldness. Its bright lights flicked on and it banged out from the barn and down our driveway toward the big road. Then, except for Aunt Greer's crying, the house and yard went quiet.

*　*　*

It took a while for Mama to soothe Aunt Greer, who cried an awful lot. As upset as she was, though, she didn't squeal on me for going into the bathroom, and I was glad for that. Even though it was only a few feet away, I would've gotten in trouble for leaving her alone.

McCall came in and sat himself at the end of my bed, and with all of us gathered that way, Mama told what happened. She said that there was a sick and infected black boy on Mr. Turpin Dunn's farm, and that the sick boy's daddy had come for Evette's daddy, and Evette's daddy had come for our daddy. It was real confusing.

"Why didn't the sick boy's daddy go fetch Mr. Dunn?" McCall asked.

Mama said, "He told us he was afraid to because of Mr. Dunn's bad temper."

McCall bounced on the bed. "I think it's on account of Mr. Dunn being in the Ku Klux Klan. Everyone knows he's —"

"McCall!" Mama scolded him.

I said, "Is he really?"

Mama shook her head. "You children mind your manners. How Mr. Dunn spends his time is his own private business."

I asked, "You think the boy's got the measles?" It was the only big disease I knew anything about.

"I don't think," Mama answered, swaying Aunt Greer back and forth like a little girl. "There're a million diseases out there."

McCall said, "He probably stepped on a nail. That'll get a person real sick."

"That's more than likely," Mama agreed.

Aunt Greer finally sat up. Sniffling and breathing so that her chest banged up and down, she whispered, "Those men gave me such a start."

"They gave us all a fright," Mama told her, patting at Aunt Greer's hair.

"Didn't scare me," McCall declared. "I was just curious."

Mama gave him her schoolteacher look. "I've had enough from you, McCall."

"Sorry," he said like he was innocent, then, secretly, he pushed his toes up under my covers and pinched my feet with them.

"McCall!" I yelped, and Mama grounded him for two days.

✳   ✳   ✳

My daddy didn't get back till breakfast time. Sleepy-looking, he trudged upstairs and into the kitchen and sat himself at the table.

Mama said, "Is the boy okay?"

My daddy shook his head. "No, he isn't."

"Is he dead?" McCall asked.

"Yes," Daddy said softly. "Yes, son, the boy died about an hour ago."

My mama was quiet before she asked, "Do they know what illness he had?"

"Yeah, it was very obvious," Daddy told her.

"What?"

"Well, to put it straight, he was beat to death."

"Oh, my land," Mama said to herself, studying the tabletop.

I stared down at my breakfast.

After a few moments, McCall declared, "Mr. Dunn did it. I heard some —"

"McCall!" Daddy cut him off. "Listen up. I don't want you saying that to anyone. You don't know what happened except for the boy died. I'm warning you right here and now."

Hurt from getting scolded so hard, McCall answered, "Yes, sir."

But I felt sure McCall was right. Mr. Turpin Dunn had killed the boy because the boy had tried to snatch a chicken. I'd heard Mr. Dunn talk about it in my daddy's store. I wanted the sheriff to come and take him to jail. I even said, "Is Sheriff McDonnell gonna come, Daddy?"

Daddy took a tiny bite from the plate of food Annie Jane had just set in front of him. "No, he won't. Reason is, it was just a black boy." He looked smack into Annie Jane's eyes. "I'm sorry," he told her, "but it's the truth. The sheriff won't look into that type of thing."

No Place on Earth
More Beautiful

On the morning that the black boy died, I went to school feeling like my brain was dangling above my head instead of being inside of it. I was so mad at Mr. Dunn that I didn't want to think about him or the little boy, who I kept picturing lying dead at the doctor's office. It seemed like the worst thing that could ever happen to a kid . . . getting beat to death.

Later, even though I didn't feel excited anymore, I skipped lunch and went down the street to the *Bennettsville Times* to show Mr. Salter my story about Great-Uncle Harvey. Pushing through the half-glass front doors, I went in slow.

Mr. Salter looked up, and said, "If it isn't Darby Carmichael, Bennettsville's favorite writer!"

"Hello, Mr. Salter."

He motioned for me to sit in a chair near his desk. "All of Bennettsville liked your article," he told me, ramming a stainy hand through his funny hair, hair as black as night.

"Thank you, Mr. Salter."

Spying my newspaper notebook, he said, "I hope that's another one. Is it?"

I said, "Yes, sir, it is. It's about my Great-Uncle Harvey, who's blind from the measles."

Mr. Salter sat on the edge of his gigantic desk. "I'm interested in the sound a that. Is it as good as the last?"

I smiled. "I think. You wanna see?"

He lifted a hand for my newspaper notebook, and I gave it to him.

I explained, "It's at the end."

Turning to the last page, he read it, then started over and reread it. Unlike my story on toads, he didn't smile once.

Finally, I asked, "You don't like it, sir?"

He looked at me. "Did you write this?"

"Yes, sir."

Studying it again, he said, "It's an altogether different type of story."

"I couldn't think of anything else to say about toads, is why."

He placed my notebook on one of his legs. "What I mean is, it's written real well. I mean, sure, it's got problems that I'll fix if I take it, but it's good. It's touching, even."

"You don't think it's cute, Mr. Salter?"

"Well, not so much." He handed my notebook to his helper, instructing him to read it. Turning back toward me, he said, "It's cute in that you care so much for your uncle, that's clear. But it's not cute like the other story." He stared at me. "To be honest, it's so different from the last story, Darby, it . . . it makes me worried that you didn't write it yourself." He gave me the kind of look that makes me squirm, the kind that my mama can give.

"The . . . the only thing different is that I got my friend Evette to help fix it up."

Chewing at a fingernail, Mr. Salter thought and thought. Then he finally said, "Can't recall whose daughter she is right offhand. What's her daddy's name?"

I hesitated. "It's Elwood."

"You know their last name?"

"Yes, sir. It's Robinson."

Mashing his chin with his fingers, he thought on that name some.

"She's . . . she's a tenant farmer's daughter who's

one of my best friends. I can see her house from my bed-room window. It's right behind Ellan."

Mr. Salter's helper handed me my notebook. As bald as a post, he smiled, and said, "It's a beautiful story. It really is."

"Thank you, sir," I answered real softly. But I was still worried they weren't going to take it.

Mr. Salter said, "Darby, was her daddy involved in what happened to that black boy from Turpin Dunn's farm?"

"I think a little bit, yes, sir."

Mr. Salter looked at the far-off ceiling. Then he stood up, walked around his desk, and flopped in his chair, which gave a good squeak. "She helped you write it?" he asked.

"Kind of, sir. She helped me smooth it up."

Smiling, he picked up a pencil. "She must be awfully smart, Darby."

"She is, sir. But I wrote it."

Mr. Salter stared at the top of his big old desk. "Darby, if I run your story, and I want to, I gotta say that your friend Evette helped. Give credit where credit's due. Now, problem is, she's black. You know? We never have run something from a black person.

In a ways, we just can't. So I'm thinking that I'm gonna say it's "written by Darby Carmichael and edited by her friend Evette." I'm not gonna give her last name, and I'm hoping people'll think she lives in Charleston or something. Is that okay? We aren't gonna lie about it. But we aren't gonna open up and say it was edited by a black girl, even if she is real smart." He winked at me.

All shook up with joy over the idea of getting Evette's name in the *Bennettsville Times,* I jumped off my chair, causing it to spill over backward onto the floor. Surprised by the noise it made, I set it straight as fast as I could, and told Mr. Salter, "Doing it like that is perfect."

Laughing, he said, "You seem happy about it."

"I am, sir. Evette's gonna be excited to get called an editor. That's why."

"Well, all right."

I placed my newspaper notebook onto his desk. "Like before, should I leave this for you to copy?"

"That's right," he said, grinning extra-wide.

"Thank you, Mr. Salter."

"Thank you. You did the work."

Thrilled, I rushed to the door. But just as I was ready to leave, Mr. Salter said, "Darby?"

I stopped. "Yes, sir?"

"Got a quick question before you head back to school."

"What?" I asked.

Rolling up his sleeves, Mr. Salter said, "Well, I was wondering what you know about that black boy on Turpin Dunn's farm? You heard anything?"

Mr. Salter's helper lifted his head and watched me like I was a fox.

Worried I'd make Daddy angry, I said, "I . . . I haven't, Mr. Salter. Why, sir?"

Lacing his fingers together, Mr. Salter pushed his hands forward so that his knuckles made sharp cracks. "Oh, I'm just thinking about things people said this morning at the Sanitary Café. Few guys were talking about it. Nothing big, mind you. They were just talking among themselves."

"My daddy said the boy died of being sick," I lied.

Mr. Salter clapped his hands together. "That's right, Darby. Anyways, you get on and tell everyone you got another story coming out."

"Thank you, sir," I called, and shot out the door and down the steps and along the street to the Murchison School's big field. The whole rest of the afternoon I felt like I was stepping on clouds. It didn't seem like my feet touched against the ground at all.

After school, I snatched my best dress-ups from the basement and ran and hid in the field so my mama wouldn't see me waiting for Evette. Then, when Evette got home, I rushed up the road to her and blurted out about both of us getting in the *Bennettsville Times*. Right off, her eyes swelled up to the size of nickels, and the two of us danced and screamed wild and crazy, kicking up a nice dirt cloud. Shortly, Evette changed, and when she came out again, she was still grinning, and her grin stayed right there as we carried my pile of dress-up clothes into the woods.

On account of it being my turn, I got to wear our favorite fancy dress. Freezing, I slid it on fast. Then I put my coat back on and smiled at how the bottom part of the dress was bright pink and shined in the sideways sun streaks. I also pulled on some old shoes that stopped fitting my mama after she had me. Alongside, Evette wore the second-best dress, which is blue with a big bow in the back that you couldn't see on account of her coat covering it over. Both of us rolled on long gloves and circled about like we were rich ladies. I said I was married to a famous husband who was a general in the army. Evette said that she wasn't married at all and that she was rich from a book she'd written about a shipwrecked family who got attacked by a polar bear.

"I read that story," I told her in a rich person's voice.

"It was good."

"Yes, it was," she agreed, trying to sound like me. "After it got published, I went and bought me two homes, plus a car, and a radio."

"You know what? We got three homes. One in France, even."

She leaned against a tree. "And after my book came out, all the boys wanted to marry me, but I told 'em I ain't interested, that I got me a writing job and they'd get in my way."

I said, "My husband, General Carmichael, he would never bother me about my job, 'cause he likes the way I do with the kids. We only have girls, and he thinks they're all the most beautiful he's ever seen in his whole life except for me. So I can do whatever I want."

"The general's nice," Evette told me.

We played that way for a long time, and it was more fun than normal because both me and Evette were going to be in the *Bennettsville Times*. We even forgot to notice the sky going dark and had to take everything off fast, then run home with the dress-ups flapping in a bundle. We laughed the whole way across the cold, windy field.

At Evette's house, she gave me a hug, and I gave her one back. "Don't forget my birthday," I said. For the first time, my mama was going to let her come.

"I ain't gonna," Evette promised.

✳   ✳   ✳

That night, after closing the store, Daddy drove out to visit the family whose boy had died. For that reason, we ate dinner later than normal. By the time Daddy got in, it was seven o'clock, and we sat down and commenced to eating right away, even though he looked half-asleep and truly sad.

Mama said, "How's the family doing?"

"Not so good," he told her. "Not so good. They're gonna bury the boy tomorrow."

"They angry?"

Daddy handed me my plate. "It's a bad situation, that's for sure."

After dinner, I had to help scrub dishes, and when I was done, I put on my coat and went out to visit my daddy on the porch, where he was drinking his headache medicine in gulps. Leaning over the big eating table, he had one of his hands jammed up under his chin, and that made his face wrinkled. Sitting next to him, I said he looked real sad, and I wished he didn't.

"I'm okay, Darby," he promised me.

"You sad for that black boy?"

"I am."

"I am, too."

Quiet, my daddy stared out over the fields and the dairy barn and all his property, which was his daddy's and his granddaddy's before that. He slurped some more headache medicine, and the extra-cold breeze pushed his hair flat to his head and made me shiver. Without even looking, he wrapped one of his strong arms around me and held me so tight to him that I could hear his stomach sputter. After a while like that, he lowered his head and said, "Darby, dear, I love this place, Ellan, and Marlboro County and my friends and the people. I love it and wouldn't wanna ever live anywhere else. But you gotta know that there're folks around here who do some God-awful things we should be ashamed of. I suppose they'll pay in heaven. But I wish I knew they would. I wish I knew that, 'cause in all the world there isn't a place more beautiful and more perfect for me and your mama and you children than right here, where we got the fields and the trees and birds and my camellia bushes. But sometimes . . . I hate it."

After speaking, Daddy got real quiet. Seated alongside him, I tried to be respectful and let his lonely words disappear into the chilly air, but, secretly, I was sort of honored and surprised that he'd said that stuff to me.

Daddy kept his head down till another breeze shook the pecan trees and got me shivering. Then, sitting straight up, he rubbed a palm on my back. "Darby, sweetie, I'm very proud of you for getting your second story in the paper. I'm as proud a daddy as there is."

"Thanks," I whispered, feeling wonderful and sad.

He said, "You worked hard."

"It didn't seem hard, is why I did it," I confessed.

"But it is hard. It's hard and rare for a child to do something like that," he told me.

I sat against him for a while. "Daddy," I finally asked, "are you still thinking about that black boy?"

"Not completely, but some," he answered.

I told him, "I'm doing it some, too."

An Argument

On Friday, which was the day before I was turning nine and having a big party, I stayed in town with Beth. Together we left school and moseyed up the street toward her house, past the tinier, pretty homes in town, which have wide, shady porches. For some reason, the whole, entire way I worried about seeing Chester, her brother. I even daydreamed that Beth left us alone for a minute, and he snuck up and kissed me smack on my cheek. It was almost nice, too, the way he did it with his eyes closed. Anyway, he is right cute except that one part of his blond hair jumps straight up and won't lay down for nothing. But in my daydream, it did. It was flat to his head.

Halfway through our walk, Beth yelled, "Darby!

Hey, Darby!"

Confused, I said, "Yeah?"

"What're you thinking about? I keep talking to you, but you aren't saying anything back. It's boring for me when you don't talk."

"Sorry," I told her.

At her house, we went around to the back door, and just as we were going in, Chester scooted past me and headed toward Mercury's pen. My eyes stuck on the back of his coat while my heart thumped like a drum. Trying to look as sweet as I could, I called after him, "Hey."

Chester didn't stop or anything. He just answered, "Hey, Darby," over his shoulder, which got me to thinking that Beth was playing a mean joke. I didn't even feel like eating the gingerbread their cook gave me.

Up in Beth's room, I said, "You want my cake?"

"Sure I do," she said. "You don't feel good?"

I didn't look at her. "I thought Chester might talk a little more."

"He would," Beth explained, "except I told him that I told you he's got a crush, and now he's embarrassed."

"You told him you told me?" I hollered. "Why'd you do that?"

"'Cause when I did it, he was being mean."

I stomped on the floor. "Now . . ." I sputtered like a

car. "Now he might not want me to help with Mercury."

"He will."

"He might not."

"He's gonna, 'cause he always says you're so nice." Beth grinned and looked evil doing it. "Darby Sinclair," she whispered after a minute, "do you got a crush on Chester or something?"

"No," I told her. "I don't. It's just that I like Mercury so much. And . . . and I also like to ride in the cart."

After that, we played with Beth's three doll babies. Each one has a smiling porcelain face and fake hair that is strapped back in a hard bun. They look like Miss Burstin, our teacher at school. We played like the one with the worst dress was sick in bed, and we got the other two to treat her nice and undress her so that her daddy could ship her to a hospital that was straight across the bedroom. When she died of coughing, our doll babies got so sad and sorrowful that they threw themselves on the pillows of Beth's bed. The thing is, while I was mashing my doll's face into some fringe, I looked back at the little crib where the undressed doll had died from coughing, and I all the sudden thought of the black boy who'd been beaten by Mr. Dunn.

I stopped making my doll squeal. I let it rest and walked over and sat in one of Beth's rocking chairs. A slice of sharp, eye-burning sun hit me on my neck and face.

"What's wrong now?" Beth asked.

I didn't know how to say it. "It's that this black boy from Mr. Dunn's farm died yesterday, and I keep imagining him stretched on a table, sorta like that doll there."

Beth looked over at the undressed doll. "If you want, we can say that we only thought she was dead."

I stared quiet at the polished floor for a while. "That'd be good."

Beth went over to the little crib. "Out of nowhere, she can cough real soft and suddenly wake up and everybody will see that she was just deep asleep."

I added, "Then she can be better and we can pretend that she's gonna get married, and we can save her from getting bit by a snake at Crooked Creek."

✻   ✻   ✻

As the sky was changing to darkness, me and Beth walked along Main Street to her daddy's office. We were hoping he might have some candy in a drawer, which he sometimes does. Streetlights were just starting up, and a few people were packing around the picture show entrance. The Carolina Theater was playing a cowboy movie that had a handsome, tough man on the poster. The Sanitary Café was full up with customers and noise. Griffin's Barbershop is alongside, and its big window was so steamy that all you could see was the outlines of folks reading newspapers. We turned the corner near the Lewis & Breeden drugstore and saw that Beth's daddy's law office had the shades drawn tight, which was strange because he never does that.

Going in, we found Mr. Fairchild talking to a black man who was squeezing and rolling a dirty hat. "Hello, Darby and Beth," Mr. Fairchild said.

"Hello, sir," we answered.

Mr. Fairchild indicated the black man. "Girls, this is Jerome Hawkins. Jerome, this here is my daughter and her friend Darby."

"Hello, missuses," the black man mumbled, and his voice sounded real familiar.

"Hey," we told him.

Mr. Fairchild said, "Girls, we're just finishing up. You mind stepping outside a minute?"

Beth leaned over his desk. "We just came to see if you have candy."

"Candy," Mr. Fairchild said. Playing shocked, he opened up a desk drawer. "You're looking for candy, you say? Why . . . why, what a coincidence. I sure do have some," he told her. He reached into a brown bag and got hold of some butterscotches.

"Thank you, sir," I said while I undid a gold wrapper.

"You're welcome, Darby."

"We're going over to her daddy's store," Beth said.

We started through the door, but before I could pass, Jerome Hawkins caught my coat sleeve, and said, "Miss Carmichael? Tell your daddy I appreciate what he done."

Confused, my eyes glued on his craggled face for a second. Then Beth pushed me outside, and we were on the busy sidewalk. The courthouse was across the street and what people call the Carmichael Block was straight ahead. We laughed and enjoyed our butterscotches, and I forgot to tell my daddy Jerome Hawkins's message.

✳   ✳   ✳

At Carmichael Dry Goods, me and Beth had Russell haul us up and down in the elevator till he said his hands were throbbing. Then we stayed upstairs and played around the shelves of dungarees and work shirts. Beth said that she was looking for a tuxedo for her pretend husband, and I was a fancy cashier and told her we had all measure of brands in silk, cotton, and wool, the silk being the fanciest since it's so hard to get and worms make it. She decided that her husband should have the best and got him the silk. After that, she searched around for a good bow tie.

"This one costs a hundred dollars," I said, lifting up a red handkerchief.

"I'll take it, plus the shiniest tuxedo shoes you got."

Taking hold of some work boots, I put them up on a tabletop. "These shine so much you might wanna put some dirt on 'em."

She declared, "Miss Carmichael, I like 'em that way, thank you."

Shortly, my daddy came upstairs alongside Mr. Fairchild, who must have walked over from his office. They settled themselves against a wall and grinned at us. After a few minutes, my daddy announced, "Darby, you tired out Russell so bad I have to give him an hour off in the morning."

"Daddy," I muttered, "are you playing?"

"Yeah, I am, sweetie."

In a little while, Beth went home with Mr. Fairchild, and me and Daddy switched off the lights and went out back to the Buick. Daddy cranked the engine. Then we got in and he steered around a corner and along Main Street toward the edge of town.

Halfway to Ellan, I asked him, "You reckon I can

talk about my birthday party yet?"

"It's so close, I don't see why not."

Excited, I twisted and looked at his shadowy face. "Did I get a present?"

"I'm sure you got something."

"I wonder what Mama's gonna do for my party."

"You'll find out." Daddy laughed and looked into his rearview mirror. A car was following close behind us, wagging back and forth so that its lights shined all around our fenders and splashed into the ditch. On the edge of Bennettsville, it sped past and got in the middle of the road, where it commenced to slow down till we had to stop.

"Why'd they do that?" I asked my daddy.

"I don't know," he said.

A minute or so went by, and a skinny man got from the car and walked toward us.

Daddy said, "Darby, honey, you stay here." Careful, he got out and met the man by our bumper. The Buick's headlights made them look like pale angels.

I rolled down my window so that I could hear, and cold air rushed against my head.

"Mr. Carmichael," the man said, tilting his hat.

"You're a long way from home," my daddy said back.

"Yeah, I am. Came here on business, if you wanna know."

"I don't."

"Sure you don't, Mr. Carmichael. But rumors is rumors, and we gotta ask questions." When the man smiled, I could see he was missing some teeth, and that gave me a shiver fit so that I had to wrap my arms across myself to stay warm.

"See, Mr. Carmichael, yer a respectable part of the Marlboro community. Why, yer a big man round here. Nobody wants nothin' ta happen ta a fella like you. That's why I gotta ask a simple question: Why'd you wanna get involved in somethin' so simple as a black boy dyin'? Why did you get involved at all, huh? What I hear is that boy, he come at Turpin, and Turpin, he didn't do nothin' but protect hisself."

My daddy leaned forward, and said, "That boy was twelve years old. If a twelve-year-old attacked me, I believe I could keep myself safe with one hand."

"That boy had a knife. You see now?"

"That boy didn't have a knife."

"Yeah, he did."

"Look, the only reason I got involved is because one of my tenant farmers woke me up and told me the boy had an infection. I didn't have any idea he'd been beaten till I saw him." I could tell Daddy was getting mad.

"You was put into a bad situation," said the skinny man. "That's for sure."

"When somebody asks for my help, if I can, I give it."

The man smiled. "Yer a good guy, Mr. Carmichael. Got a family that goes to church and you keeps yer farm runnin' in hard times. And, I'll tell you, helpin' some-one's fine. Helpin' anyone is. But we got ourselves another situation altogether. Now, if a black man was ta ask you for a lawyer, you wouldn't help him get that, would you? You wouldn't give one of them that sorta powerful information?"

My daddy took a small step closer to the man. Fear-ful they were gonna wrastle each other, I shrunk down and curled in a knot on the seat. Still, I listened as hard as I could.

Daddy said, "Now, hold on. Yesterday Mr. Hawkins asked me who he could see about legal coun-sel, and I told him. He asked, and I told him. That's all. I gave him Mr. Fairchild's name, and Mr. Fairchild came and informed me not twenty minutes ago that he can't be any help. So except for you threatening me, I think it's all over. Don't you?"

The man didn't say anything.

"Don't you?" my daddy shouted at him.

The man raised his voice back. "Mr. Carmichael, don't you get disrespectful with me, 'specially after what you done!"

Daddy said, "I'll get as disrespectful as I want. That's exactly what I'm gonna do. You stop me on the road like this again, and I'm gonna get real disrespectful. I'm gonna get downright nasty."

Laughing, the man said, "Oh, yer a big fella, Mr. Carmichael, but you couldn't shake no bullet, I don't think. You take a look in that back window of my car, and you'll see I didn't come alone. The Ku Klux Klan don't ever come alone. So next time you get ta feelin' so friendly, you best consider the cost. Y'understand?"

My daddy didn't talk.

"You hear me okay, Mr. Carmichael?"

Daddy opened his car door, and he got in. He got the Buick rolling forward and around the man and the car that was sitting in the middle of the road. After a few minutes of driving, he said, "Darby? Darby, sweetheart, it's okay. Those boys just needed directions. They're from Columbia, and they lost their way, was all."

I started to cry. I couldn't stop. Bawling, I said, "I . . . I heard what he said, Daddy! I heard him say he was from the Ku Klux Klan and how you might get shot by a bullet."

✻   ✻   ✻

Upstairs, hidden from Aunt Greer, Mama squeezed me hard and told me that nothing bad was going to come of what happened. But I couldn't stop crying. It was terrible. I didn't want my daddy to die, and I didn't want to, either. "I . . . I hate Mr. Dunn," I sobbed.

My mama rocked me good. She said, "Mr. Dunn probably didn't have anything to do with what happened."

Placing a hand on my head, Daddy told me, "Darby, they're all bluster and nothing more. The Klan is all bluster."

"What's *bluster* mean?"

"Means hot air," Mama explained.

"That's what they're full of," Daddy declared, "just like a balloon. Besides, I promise you, we're gonna be fine. I wouldn't ever let something happen to you, your brother, or Mama."

"You forgot about Aunt Greer," Mama joked.

He laughed. "That's right, Aunt Greer, too."

Smiling a little, I said, "How about your camellia bushes?"

A grin came on his face. "Now you're playing dirty. I wouldn't allow anyone or anything to lay a hand on those."

Smiling wider, I snuffled. "Daddy, I swiped a bud

for my hair on Monday."

"Oh, I know you did," he said. "You always take them from the bush over by the smokehouse."

Surprised that he knew about that, I couldn't help feeling better.

My Birthday

When I woke up on the morning of my birthday, what happened the night before seemed like a scary dream that wouldn't melt away. Still, I tried not to think too hard on the skinny man with missing teeth. Whenever I started to, I focused on turning nine and how I was going to have cake and get some presents after lunch. That made me feel better.

Shaking from the cold, I slipped from my bed and rushed over to the fire that was snapping and sizzling on the andirons in my hearth. Freezing, I snuck so close I nearly climbed in. When I was warm, I rushed to the wardrobe and got my best dress from a hanger and slid it on as quick as I could. Then I found some socks and buckled on my Sunday shoes. Pulling a sweater around me, I charged downstairs to the warm kitchen.

"Hey, Annie Jane," I said, and went straight to the stove, which I commenced to leaning against.

"Happy birthday, youngin." Annie Jane was poking at strips of sizzling bacon with a fork. She wore a kerchief on her head, and her dress was one of Mama's old ones with real small flowers all over it and a tearing hemline.

"You know what Mama's got planned for today?" I asked her.

"I ain't saying."

I leaned flat against the oven's warm sides. "Annie Jane, what kinda cake are you making me?"

"Your favorite."

"Chocolate?"

"Yas, ma'am."

Inside the stove, logs roared. "Do you think I gotta eat breakfast, or can I save up for my party?"

Annie Jane bobbed her head from side to side. "Oh, I'm sure you gots ta eat somethin'."

"Maybe just a little bacon?"

"Full meal is what I 'spect your tummy be calling for."

Warmed up, I wandered away from the stove and over to the window. I looked down on our outbuildings and the Darby and Beth School. "I wish eleven-thirty would hurry up," I told her.

"Let's see," she replied real easy-like, making a show of turning all the way around and staring at the wind-up clock, "you gots yourself a three-hour wait. You best figure out what to do so it don't take forever."

Gazing at our sunny backyard, I was thinking, *Three whole hours!* when my daddy sauntered in for breakfast. Sitting down, he didn't talk right away. Then, after gulping down a warm glass of milk, he dabbed his mouth with his napkin and gave me a good looking-over, like a teacher. "You okay, Darby?" he finally asked.

"It's my birthday," I answered, and, directly, my head swam with pictures of the skinny Klan man and Daddy, looking like they were gonna grab each other. I trembled and smiled. "Right now, I'm real happy 'cause I'm already nine," I told him.

He nodded. "Yes, you are. The only reason I ask is I don't want you worrying about last night."

"I ain't," I blurted.

"*I'm not,*" he said, correcting my talk.

"I'm not," I repeated.

Daddy scrunched his napkin into his lap. "That sort of thing can be scary, Darby, but you should know it doesn't bother me a bit. Those boys aren't so interested in us."

From the side of my eye, I could see Annie Jane

watching and wondering what Daddy was meaning. "I know," I told him, wanting to take an eraser and rub the Ku Klux Klan man out of my head like lines of chalk on a blackboard.

✳   ✳   ✳

I spent the morning out back, kicking the basketball against a fence and pole-vaulting. Every so often, a black family stopped by the Grab, which is this little building inside our backyard where tenant farmers can shop without going all the way to town. They come by and knock on our back door, and Mama or Aunt Greer runs out and helps them get supplies like flour or eggs or things of that sort. Then we mark it in a book, and my daddy takes it from their wages.

Tenant farmers came and went from the Grab, and I watched the families until McCall shuffled out and we played basketball. Like usual, though, McCall got upset that I kept beating him, so he didn't play too long before he went back inside. Bored, I walked into the front yard and skipped beneath our flagpole trees, kicking up pine needles in the grass. Traipsing all the way out to the highway, I ran across the cold, blowy road and dragged my feet along for fun, sending dust puffing into the air. Then, for no reason, I wandered into our big red barn that sometimes seems like a church with a steeple. I climbed up into the hayloft, where I stared out the loft door with its pulley and hoist above. Leaning, I peered across the fields. I saw past way-off tenant homes that looked more like crumpled woodpiles. I saw turkey vultures circling in the cold sky the way they do. I saw a line of trees that ends one of our smallest fields and starts Mr. Dunn's property. And there was Mr. Dunn's house, so little, as if ants lived in it. It wasn't dark or mean or even real seeming. It didn't look like a little kid would die there or like the owner would belong to the Ku Klux Klan, either. Nervous, I backed up and fell over a hay bale. Then I thought that it had to be near about eleven-thirty, so I ran back to Ellan as fast as I could. When I got there, I saw that I still had an hour and a half to wait.

❊   ❊   ❊

For my birthday party, Mama had made a fright show downstairs. She'd set up little booths and blankets all over. You reached your hand into a hole to feel a wolf's brain or a witch's tooth or monkey eyeballs, and that got all of us screaming so that for a while my party was crazy. It was gross fun, and it wasn't till afterward that we found out the stuff we touched wasn't real. The wolf's brain was an oyster, and the witch's tooth was an arrowhead and the monkey eyeballs, they were two pickled quail eggs.

Later, out in front of Ellan, as we took sticks and tried to burst open a bag full of candy and tiny presents, Sissy surprised me by telling Evette to fetch her a drink, which Evette did. Boy, that got me mad at the both of them. "You aren't here to help," I told Evette. To Sissy, I said, "She's our friend and isn't gonna get stuff for anyone but herself." But that didn't stop anybody from treating her different.

Even though it was a little cold out, Mama and Aunt Greer had set four small tables in the backyard. They were real pretty, too, with white cloths draped over the tops and nice cups and glasses arranged right. Also, because I was the birthday girl, I got to choose who I wanted to sit alongside me, and I decided on Evette and Beth even though it wasn't exactly proper for a white girl to eat alongside a black girl. I didn't care, though. During lunch I even told them, "I wish for my birthday that we were friends and that the three of us would do anything for each other. I wish we were pretend sisters."

Evette answered, "Beth don't wanna be my sister."

Beth gave a shrug, causing the shoulders of her coat

to rise up beside her pretty ears, which are the other things about her I want.

"She's saying she doesn't mind being pretend sisters," I informed Evette.

Beth said, "I'm not saying that."

I gave her a stern stare. "You should, 'cause Evette's so nice and you are, and it doesn't make any sense that we wouldn't be pretend sisters."

"Sure it does," Evette told me. "It's 'cause I'm black."

"No it isn't," I told her, but right off I knew she was right.

Quiet for a little bit, Beth pushed a piece of cake around with a spoon. Then she finally spoke. "If it's what you want, Darby, just for this afternoon I'll play sisters."

Smiling, I told her, "Thanks," and I swung about and made big eyes at Evette.

She bulged hers back. "I suppose you wants me to play like we're sisters, too?"

I told her, "It's my birthday." Taking up both of their hands, I said, "We're playing sisters."

Sitting at the other tables, my friends looked at us.

"We're playing sisters," I announced again.

Sissy frowned. "How can you be sisters? She's black."

Angry, I told her, "We're just playing, is how."

After cake, Mama and Aunt Greer got some games going. We pinned paper tails on the outline of a donkey and did musical chairs with a phonograph. We were sitting in the cold grass, playing hot potato, when Boog's daddy arrived to take him and Shoog, who was his neighbor, home. Then Helen's brother drove up and carried her and Jack-Henry back into town. A few minutes later, Beth's parents, Mr. and Mrs. Fairchild, bounced down the driveway in their Cadillac, pulling up next to the Grab. Getting out, Mrs. Fairchild came over to us while Mr. Fairchild waved and went into Ellan. Watching the door shut behind him, I wondered if he wanted to talk to my daddy about the Klan man. I stared at the back side of the house for a few minutes. Then I forgot and listened to Mrs. Josephine Fairchild's funny story about one of her birthday parties when she was little. She told about how her daddy had made up an extra-large pot of Brunswick stew, and their dog found it and pushed the top off and tried climbing in before it spilled on top of him.

"Did your dog get burnt?" Evette asked.

"Luckily, it wasn't steaming hot."

"If it was, he might've cooked," I said.

"You're right," she agreed.

Mrs. Fairchild started in on another story about her

dog, and by the time she was finishing up, my daddy and Mr. Fairchild came out the back door and moseyed in a circle around us, stopping by the laundry house. They began laughing.

I peeked over at Beth and smiled.

She smiled back.

Turning, Beth's mama said to me, "Darby, I nearly forgot to tell you. I loved your article in the *Bennettsville Times*."

"You did?" I asked.

"It was exceptionally sweet," she declared.

"Thank you, ma'am," I told her. "I got another one coming out next week. But I don't think it's gonna be sweet. It's different 'cause Evette helped fix it up and . . . and . . ." I sputtered to a stop. My heart sunk because I'd just given away the secret me and Mr. Salter were keeping.

"Evette," Mama said, turning toward my friend, "you helped her write about Great-Uncle Harvey?"

Shaking her head, Evette answered, "No, ma'am. I just fixed things when she asked me to. My aunt's been writing for a newspaper in New York, so I've wanted to write. I wanted to since I was little."

Mama looked back at me. "Is that why you got the itch to write articles, because of Evette?"

For a minute or two, I considered not telling the

117

truth and even thought about running over to my daddy. But I didn't do either. I stood my ground and repeated to myself that newspaper girls are supposed to tell the truth.

I said, "Yes, Mama, she's how I got the idea. I liked what Evette told me about newspaper girls, and I was thinking that if I don't ever have any money and can't ever afford new dresses and jewelry, then I might wanna do something like that."

My mama turned toward Evette. "I'm impressed you've got such a fine grasp of the language."

"I guess I just do," Evette whispered.

Mrs. Fairchild touched Evette on the head. "I think it's wonderful that you want to be a writer."

"Thank you, ma'am," she answered bashfully.

Beth tugged at her mama's dress. "Me and Evette and Darby, we played like we were sisters today."

Mrs. Fairchild nodded. "Do you want to be a writer now?"

"We didn't talk about that," Beth admitted.

Nervous, I watched Mama's face soften to the notion that I'd copied Evette. Like everyone in Marlboro County, my mama has a lot of respect for Mrs. Fairchild, and if Mrs. Fairchild believes something is okay, everyone usually decides that way with her.

"So, Darby, how was your party?" Mrs. Fairchild

asked me.

"Oh, it was fun. Mama set up a fright show and we had games and ice cream and cake and such, and we played tag. But I haven't opened my presents yet so that other kids don't get jealous."

Laughing, Mrs. Fairchild pushed some of her pretty curls behind an ear.

My daddy and Mr. Fairchild walked over. Tilting his hat, Mr. Fairchild said, "Hello, Greer and Big Darby and Sissy. Happy birthday, Little Darby." Then he surprised me and stuck a hand on one of Evette's shoulders. Squatting down, he smiled at her. "Darby's daddy just told me you're Elwood Robinson's daughter. Is that right?"

Evette's eyes became wide and worried. "Yes, sir."

"Darby's daddy thinks the world of your father."

"Yes, sir."

"I got a question for you."

"Okay, sir."

"How does your daddy know Mr. Hawkins, the man whose boy died the other night?"

She shrugged. "They's friends from church, sir. My daddy and Mr. Hawkins collects the money in baskets and sometimes they go to church at night to discuss things."

"Did you know Mr. Hawkins's boy?"

"Yes, sir. His name was Devin, and he was older. He was nice to me, but once I saw him pull his sister's hair."

Mr. Fairchild nodded and let go of Evette's shoulder. Standing, he smoothed out the top of his pants. He told her, "It was a sad thing that happened."

Evette said, "Yes, sir."

✳   ✳   ✳

When everyone was gone and Annie Jane was doing dishes, I opened my presents from Mama and Daddy and Aunt Greer while McCall sat nearby and watched. "Hurry up," he egged me, " I wanna see if I like anything."

I said, "It doesn't matter 'cause I won't let you have it."

Altogether there were three presents, and I picked the biggest one first. Tearing it open, I found a new wool sweater that Mama had knit me. Holding it in the air, I imagined myself wearing it to school. "It's so pretty," I told her. Getting up, I gave her a big hug. The next gift I opened was wrapped in a kitchen cloth. As I undid it, I recognized that it was a little plaster sculpture of a horse with Robert E. Lee, the famous Southern general from the Civil War, alongside him. Since before I could recollect, my daddy had kept that teeny sculpture on his desk at Carmichael Dry Goods. On account of the horse being so proud and handsome, I always liked it. When I'd sit in his office, I'd pretend that the horse was a unicorn and Robert E. Lee was a princess.

"Thank you, Daddy," I told him, getting up and giving him a hug.

"I know how much you liked it."

"Yeah," I said, feeling dizzy from happiness.

The last thing I got was a pecan pie that Aunt Greer had made me.

"Can I have some?" I asked.

"Not till after dinner," Aunt Greer said.

That night while tucking me in bed, Mama said, "Was it a good day, sweetheart?"

"Yeah," I told her, looking into her round, friendly face. Unless she's mad, she's so sweet-looking that you just want to climb into her arms and have her hold you tight and delicate. Sometimes, it seems impossible that she was considered one of the hardest and meanest teachers at the Murchison School. But everyone says that it's true, that when she first got to town, she was serious and difficult and didn't want anything to do with the locals, including my daddy. I guess that changed after he asked her to marry him.

"Mama, are you angry about me wanting to be a newspaper girl?"

She laughed. "No, Darby. Newspaper writing isn't ladylike, but it's not a horrible thing for a girl to try her hand at."

"Evette's real smart," I told her. "If she wasn't black, she'd be a genius."

"I suppose."

"Mama," I said, "why do you think Mr. Fairchild asked her all those questions?"

She shook her head. "Who knows?"

I said, "Mama, I love my sweater, and the fright show was perfect."

"It's my pleasure to do those things," she told me, tucking the covers around my shoulders.

In a Silent Movie

On the Monday after my birthday, Daddy came home from work with the *Bennettsville Times*. Excited, he showed me and Mama and Aunt Greer my new article. I called Annie Jane over to see, and the four of us crowded around Daddy. Looking between his hands, I saw my story at the bottom of the front page. In big letters it said: "Living Without Sight." In small letters it said, "Another article by Marlboro County's favorite columnist, Little Darby Carmichael, with editorial assistance from Evette."

I asked my daddy, "What's a columnist?"

He answered, "It's a newspaper writer who writes personal opinions and stories."

"I'm a columnist kinda newspaper writer then?"

"Sure are." Aunt Greer laughed.

I asked, "Did you like my story, Daddy?"

"I was left breathless," he declared. "It's really an accomplishment."

"You think?" I asked, and started jumping up and down.

Annie Jane told me, "Congratulations, child."

Mama finished reading and shook her head. "Amazing," she said, her throat and eyes clogged with tears. She reached over and held my cheeks in her hands. Letting go, she gave me a nice soft hug. "I'm proud of you. You've got a special gift. You certainly do."

McCall walked in, and I yapped, "My new columnist came out."

"You mean your column?" he snapped back.

I was confused.

Aunt Greer explained, "A columnist writes a column."

"So what I did is called a column?"

"Yeah, love," she told me as she read.

I turned back to McCall. "Everyone thinks my column's real good."

"Who cares," he mumbled.

"McCall!" Mama barked at him. "Be good!"

Playing innocent, he declared, "I'm being good."

I asked my mama, "Can I go show Evette?"

"Right now?"

"It'll only be a second, Mama. Please?"

Staring at me, she didn't try to hide her frustration. "You don't dawdle, Darby," she said sharply, "and take King."

The nice thing was, when Evette saw her name alongside mine, she got so excited she gave me a hug that nearly cracked my back. It was perfect.

*   *   *

A lot of people liked my second article more than the first, including the teachers I eat lunch with. They praised me about ten times, which was something I didn't mind. Plus, my daddy said that everyone who went into his store gushed over it. At home and at school I was feeling pretty important until, on the Thursday after my birthday, while Miss Burstin wrote on the blackboard, Beth gave me a note. Unfolding it, I read, "You got to come home with me. Mercury is so sad for not seeing you for almost two weeks. That's what Chester said."

Thinking about that goat, I wrote back, "Are you playing?" But Beth never got my question. While my head was down, Miss Burstin had walked away from the blackboard and was standing in front of me. She grabbed up my note and scolded me good. "Darby Carmichael, I'd like to think that you of all people would try and set a good example for others." Ripping the paper into a hundred pieces, she sprinkled it into the garbage can.

When school was over, I got up and rushed for the parking lot and our Chevrolet. I wanted to go straight home and hide under the sweet, blue sky of our farm. But Beth caught up with me downstairs. "Darby, aren't you gonna come make Mercury happy?" she asked.

Breathing hard, I stared at her. "Is that really true about him?"

"Yeah, it is," she promised. "Even Chester said you gotta come make his goat feel better."

I wanted to leave, but I knew I couldn't. I liked Mercury so much I was stuck. "Okay, I'll stay."

"Mercury's gonna be glad," Beth told me.

Walking to her house, I explained that because I was semifamous for writing articles in the paper, I felt especially bad about getting caught passing notes.

Beth told me to stop worrying.

"You think?"

"It's true. Miss Burstin shouldn't've said you should set a good example. That wasn't very nice. You're still just a kid."

I thought about it but couldn't exactly decide if Beth was right. We walked on some more, and I asked, "Did you like my birthday?"

She nodded. "It was nice."

"You didn't like Evette, though, did you?"

"I like her all right."

"She's smart and funny."

Beth didn't answer.

"You should hear her tell stories about her brothers. Once she said they were walking down a dirt road, and they passed a snake who was sitting in a ditch, and her little brother stayed behind and picked it up and swang it like a rope. He tossed it around their older brother's neck, and their older brother nearly screamed his head off from fright. He was worried it was a poisonous snake. As soon as he found out it wasn't, he wrastled their little brother into the dirt and made him eat a handful."

"Ugh, I woulda fainted if somebody threw a snake around my neck," Beth declared.

"Me, too," I told her.

She laughed.

"You see how fun Evette is?"

She didn't say anything.

At Beth's house, Chester stayed in his room while we brushed Mercury's soft coat. Stepping in place,

Mercury seemed happy I was there. I asked Beth, "Do you really think he missed me?"

"That's what Chester thought."

"Good," I said, scratching the area between Mercury's eyes and down his big nose.

When we were finished brushing Mercury, we went inside. A few minutes later, Chester and Mercury clip-clopped down the roadway and disappeared around the side of the house. Watching them go, I wished Beth's brother would start talking to me again. I missed hearing him explain how to gig frogs and play football. Also, he knows the best ghost stories and tells them in a strange voice that makes the hair on my neck stand as straight as pins.

Playing dolls, me and Beth decided that the worst-dressed one went crazy and the two prettier ones had to send her to an insane hospital. After a while, the prettier dolls came to visit her, but the boss at the hospital was so mean that he wouldn't let them talk. The two pretty dolls could hear the worst-dressed one crying for help inside the gate, and it was on account of her crying that the pretty dolls broke her out of the hospital and hid her under Beth's bed.

After playing, Beth and me had some lemonade and walked down to Crooked Creek. We tossed stones to see who could throw the farthest. Beth won, but she didn't say anything because we don't like to pick winners. Then we went back up the hill and walked toward Carmichael Dry Goods.

Going along, though, Boog and Shoog ran by us, stopped, and came back. Excited, Boog said, "Beth, did you hear somebody just threw a brick through your daddy's office window?"

"By mistake?" Beth asked.

"Course not," he told her.

Beth started trotting, and I chased after her. With Boog and Shoog right behind us, we shot around the Lewis & Breeden drugstore and saw all the people and the sheriff alongside Mr. Fairchild's window. As I searched the crowd for my daddy, my eyes stopped on Mr. Dunn, who stood in back with his giant arms crossed.

Talking with the sheriff, Mr. Fairchild was pointing at the glass on the ground and the busted blinds that were hanging crumpled.

Behind me, Boog whispered, "Everyone around here is saying it was the KKK."

Spinning about, I looked right at him.

He whispered, "That's short for the Ku Klux Klan."

I already knew that, and my heart nearly stopped. I turned back to watch Beth weave through the crowd to her daddy. Hugging him, she started crying so that handsome Mr. Fairchild crouched down and lifted her up.

The crowd grew bigger and Mr. Fairchild kept talking to Sheriff McDonnell. Finally, when they were done, people came around and patted Mr. Fairchild's shoulders, wishing him well. He smiled and laughed and put Beth down. Shaking hands with friends, he lifted his head and was blotting his face with a handkerchief when he spotted Mr. Dunn. From where I was standing, it seemed like Mr. Dunn's sharp chin hypnotized Mr. Fairchild or something, because Beth's daddy started toward him right off. Yelling things that I couldn't hear, because I couldn't hear anything for some reason, Mr. Fairchild pushed through the crowd. Like stuff happening in a silent movie, he struggled to get hold of Mr. Dunn as Mr. Dunn worked to grab him. Both of them looked crazy.

With a hand on his gun, the sheriff calmed the crowd. Then he must have told us all to go home, because everyone started leaving. Alongside Boog and Shoog, I walked like a zombie across the street to the Carmichael Block.

In front of my daddy's store, my hearing came back. Shoog scratched into the armpit of his coat, and mumbled, "Wonder what that note said?"

"What note?" I asked, feeling only half-awake.

"The note that was strung to that brick."

"There was a note?"

"God, Darby," Boog hollered, "you got your ears packed with wax? Everyone was talkin' about it."

"Well, I didn't hear anything." Turning away, I went into the store. From behind the cash register, my daddy looked at me.

"Darby, sweetheart, what's all the fuss? People've been rushing past the store for ten minutes."

I answered. "Somebody threw a brick through Mr. Fairchild's window."

Rightly surprised, my father thought on that before asking, "Anything else?"

"People were saying it was the Ku Klux Klan."

Daddy shook his head. "Good Lord."

"Boog and Shoog said a note was attached to a brick, but I didn't hear what it said."

"Hope this don't tear Marlboro County in half."

"What do you mean?" I asked.

"Nothing," he told me. But I knew it was something.

✳   ✳   ✳

After dinner, our telephone rang, which was real rare. Daddy answered it in the hallway. Shortly, his feet clicked on the stairs and he stood in my doorway.

"Darby?" he said, holding a glass of water.

"Yes, Daddy?"

"You get to have Beth stay for the weekend."

Excited, I put down my book. "Really?" I said, smiling.

"Yeah," he answered weakly. Then, looking like he was thinking real hard, he turned away.

Walking Mosquito Hawks

On Friday after school, me and Beth sat in the back seat of the Chevrolet and watched McCall's friends leap off the car. Once we were unloaded of boys, we picked up speed, flicking up rocks against the fenders. Outside of town, we shot along between the fields and distant, distant trees that remind me of pussy willows brushing back and forth. Driving, McCall glanced into the rearview mirror and asked Beth a question. "Are your parents scared for you to stay home?"

She answered, "It's just that they wanna know who threw the brick."

"What'd the note say?"

"Daddy didn't tell."

McCall drove on, then asked, "You think your

daddy could punch out Mr. Dunn?"

"Yeah," Beth told him. "I expect he could beat up anybody 'cause he boxed when he went to the Citadel college."

To be nice, I grabbed one of Beth's hands.

She squeezed mine back.

McCall asked, "You think it was the KKK?"

Beth shrugged. "I suppose."

McCall banged a palm against the steering wheel. "Do you know what your daddy done to make 'em mad?"

"I don't," she answered, her voice so soft it caught up in the breeze and seemed nearly to disappear.

At Ellan, me and Beth marched up to my room and changed from our school clothes. Collecting some books and paper off my shelf, we carried them downstairs, where Annie Jane gave us sugar cookies for a snack. Pulling on our coats, we dashed down to the backyard, where we went into the Darby and Beth School. Shutting the door, we swept the floor. Then we wiped down two bashed school desks we pretended our imaginary students sat in. Up at the front of the class, we put the books and paper on a rickety table and got ready to play like we were in a schoolhouse full of kids.

Taking a piece of chalk, Beth wrote arithmetic

problems on a shard of broken blackboard.

With a stick, I tapped on one of the desks. "Attention. Attention, class. Hey! Hey now, Rodney Phipps, you best listen when I'm talking. You hear? You of all people. You didn't do your arithmetic again, so you shouldn't oughta be wasting your time."

"That's right," Beth said, "you're gonna fail now. We got no choice. As hard as your mama and daddy work to bring you up right, it's a shame you're letting 'em down."

Circling one of the desks, I talked in a sweet voice. "Now, Emily, you're a different story. Last night I looked over your test from yesterday, and I see that you got everything right. Isn't that something? See what studying your homework can do for you? It can make you real smart."

Beth said, "Both me and Miss Carmichael are real proud of you. You're sitting pretty." Turning around fast, she scowled like she smelled something crummy. "On the other hand, Timothy-Lester, you don't ever seem to learn your multiplication tables. They aren't all that hard, but you can't ever get 'em."

I declared, "There's a real simple reason, Miss Fairchild. It's 'cause he daydreams too much. He's always looking out the window."

"He always is," Beth agreed.

We played that way for about a half hour, scolding and complimenting our ten imaginary students whose names we'd made up when we were little kids. Then we heard Ellan's back door open and shut, and, after a few seconds, McCall tapped at our schoolhouse. Poking his head in, he whispered, "You wanna go with me to spy on Mr. Dunn's farm?"

"No," I said, shocked he'd do something like that. To me, that whole place was getting more and more creepy.

But Beth put down her piece of chalk and answered, "I wanna, yeah."

So I was stuck. On account of Beth being a guest, I had to do what she wanted.

✳   ✳   ✳

Hurrying catty-corner toward the woods, the three of us passed into the trees and snuck along behind bushes till we got to the drainage ditch between Mr. Dunn's and my daddy's property. Stopping, we looked way up the long, bush-lined ditch. The highway was in the distance, and I could see people and mules in the fields beyond.

Since we were stopped, I tried to explain why we

shouldn't go spying on Mr. Dunn. I said, "He could sic a dog on us and beat us to bits and shoot at us and call the sheriff and —"

McCall stopped me. "He can't do nothing like that stuff. He can't knock us around. Besides, we'll stay on Carmichael property."

Beth whispered, "My daddy thinks he threw the brick at his window."

McCall turned, and told her, "We should try to see him doing something illegal."

She nodded.

Climbing down into the ditch, we scampered alongside the still water. Slipping and sliding, my shoes got caked with mud while the hem of my white dress turned orange. Ahead of me, Beth's dress was the same way. McCall's knickers and socks were plastered with clay. Stepping over big roots and fallen tree trunks, we kept our eyes on Mr. Dunn's side of the ditch till we got so we could see the top of his house. From there, we followed McCall up the Carmichael side of the bank and scampered in behind thick bushes with leaves that look like fans. Peeking through thin spots, it surprised me that Mr. Dunn's place didn't seem scary or bad or anything. Instead, it was clean and white and glowing in the sunlight.

Shimmying up a tree, McCall got into its branches

so that he could see better. He whispered down, "I got my eye on the chicken coop where he caught that boy stealing."

One of the help, carrying a washtub full of water, came out from the back of the house. She dumped it onto the dusty ground. Wiping at her head with a wrist, she turned extra-slow and went back inside.

A dog barked from behind one of Mr. Dunn's out-buildings, and I heard other noises. Following the sound, I spotted a big cage with two peacocks in it. One opened up its tail feathers, but instead of being beautiful, the feathers looked like burned stalks of grass. A calico cat scampered by, and a black man came from between some buildings, hauling wood toward the rear of Mr. Dunn's place. Stopping, he looked over toward us. He kept his eyes scanning for a time before he quit and went on.

"Did he see us?" Beth asked me softly.

"Naw," I told her. "Some people can tell when they're getting looked at, but he didn't see us." After a while I asked, "How long do you wanna stay?"

"Till we see Mr. Dunn."

"We might not. He might go in the front door."

"That's true."

"His house doesn't look so mean, huh?"

"Not like I thought," she admitted.

"He's still got an outhouse and a hand water pump in the backyard."

"Guess he's old-fashioned," Beth whispered.

As quick as a squirrel, McCall scampered down from the tree. "I didn't see nothing good," he told us. "They must be off somewheres. Let's go home."

＊　　＊　　＊

During the night, it rained. In the morning the air was hot again. The weather changes a lot around here. Sometimes the summer doesn't give up till after Christmas. Following breakfast, me and Beth went outside and set up penny peeks before getting out my pole-vaulting stick. I tried to show her how to do it a few times, but she wasn't any good. She kept trying and trying, but she couldn't swing her legs over the tiniest fence.

"Let's stop," I said to her.

"Okay," she agreed.

I could tell she was a little sad, so I asked, "Are you worried about your daddy and mama?"

"A little."

"Sorry," I told her.

"It's okay," she said. Then she walked close to me,

and whispered, "Also . . . also, do you think McCall likes me a little?" Dropping her eyes toward the ground, Beth played with her dress against her knees.

I told her, "Everybody thinks you're pretty."

She got red in the face.

Then I heard Evette calling for me. Excited, I told Beth, "Come on this way." I started running and she chased close behind me. Veering around the Grab, we passed beneath the pecan trees and out into the fields, where Evette was standing. "Hey!" I hollered, skipping up and down, waving.

Evette hollered back.

When we got to her, I said, "Beth's spending the weekend at Ellan 'cause somebody threw a brick at her daddy's office window."

"That ain't very nice," Evette said, but she didn't sound like she even cared.

I said, "It wasn't nice at all. And you know what people are saying? They're saying it was the Ku Klux Klan. Isn't that scary?"

Beth declared, "I don't know why they're bothering my daddy. He's important in town."

Evette looked down at her shoes. "Bet I know why."

Beth stared at her. "If you know, you should say."

Evette hesitated. "It's . . . it's 'cause he might take Mr. Dunn to court for killing Devin Hawkins, that boy he was asking about. That's what my daddy was saying."

Beth stood quiet for what seemed like five minutes. Then tears started from her eyes.

"What?" I asked her.

She didn't want to say and turned her back and looked at Ellan.

"You gotta tell me," I told her.

Wiping her cheeks, Beth blubbered, "If . . . if that's all it is . . . if this is because my daddy might take Mr. Dunn to court, I wish he'd go back to his normal lawyering. Until he started helping Mr. Hawkins, he never had a brick thrown at him, and I never had to get outa my house on account of them being scared some-body might hurt me."

✳   ✳   ✳

The three of us walked slowly through the cotton fields, our feet digging up the wet dirt like we were mules. Near the edge of the woods, we looked back and saw the dairy barn and, mostly hidden behind it, the hog house. "Our swing is back here," I explained to Beth. "McCall made it so it goes over a gully. That's why it can seem like you go so high off the ground."

"McCall made it?" she asked.

I tried not to smile. "Yeah, he did."

Evette told Beth, "We takes turns swinging. We makes it a game sometimes. We say you gotta switch the way you do it. Sometimes we say you gotta hold on from the bottom. Sometimes we say you gotta stand on the plank. It's so we don't get bored. If one of us gets too chicken to try somethin', the other wins. That's how we play it."

I said, "Once we were gonna swing to the other side of the gully and jump off, but we were too scared. If we missed, we might've tumbled in and broke our necks or legs even."

Doing a cartwheel, Evette stopped and wiped her hands clean on a cotton plant. "Nearby the swing is a tree where we keeps us thread and cloth for catching mosquito hawks. You done that before?"

Beth shrugged. "I don't even know what a mosquito hawk is."

"It's a dragonfly," I told her. "Me and Evette call 'em mosquito hawks."

Beth stopped and smiled like we were fooling her. "How do you catch a dragonfly with string?"

Evette explained, "You drop the cloth on 'em, then you tie the string round their tail parts. When they're good and roped, we walk 'em like little dogs, 'cept they fly."

Beth smiled. "Really?"

"Yup," Evette told her.

After swinging for more than an hour, we fetched the thread and cloth and went back out to the fields, where we hunted till we each had a mosquito hawk tied to a thread and fluttering above us. We let them go where they wanted, chasing behind so that after a half-hour Evette was clear over by the ditch separating Mr. Dunn's property from ours and Beth was near the roadway, while mine was so lazy it went in big, zigzaggy circles, like a saw blade.

After a while, we dragged our mosquito hawks back to the edge of the woods and let them go. Beth called, "Bye-bye!" to hers, so me and Evette did, too.

Walking back to hide our thread and cloth, I declared, "My mosquito hawk wasn't so good. It didn't go anywhere."

"Me and Evette had good ones," Beth bragged.

"Yeah," Evette agreed.

I stopped and gawked at both of them. "See, y'all, now it's like we're sisters."

Beth nodded. "Maybe a little."

After putting the cloth and thread away, we sat down beneath the swing and told one another what we wanted to be when we were older. Beth said, "I wanna marry a prince or a rich man and become a schoolteacher for real little kids. I wanna teach 'em arithmetic. Plus I wanna have three girls when I get old enough, but I don't want any boys. If I do, I'll give 'em away."

"Same here," I declared, wiping the sweatiness from my head.

"I don't mind boys," Evette said. "My brothers're so dumb they always make me laugh."

I said, "I wanna marry a prince, and I wanna be rich and have nice dresses and pretty hair. But now I also wanna be a newspaper girl. I wanna always write my newspaper column about things because it's fun when people tell you how good it is."

Evette said, "Me, I just wanna be a newspaper writer and have a house in New York City like my aunt and uncle. Plus, I wants me a fancy car that my butler can drive so I can come down here to see my mama and daddy. Thing is, I don't care if I ever gets married. It don't matter to me so much."

"You don't want kids?" Beth asked.

Evette shrugged. "Not so much."

"Why not?"

Evette stuck a finger through a big hole in her dress. Then she found another hole and even two more after that. "If . . . if I could have kids that was treated like white kids, I might want 'em okay. But black kids round here don't got much chance to do nothing and not much

144

chance to own nothing, either."

Beth asked, "What stuff don't you guys have?"

Evette lifted a finger that was stuck through one of the holes in her dress. She pointed off toward the tenant house her daddy rented from my daddy. "We don't got a real home. We don't got good clothes. We don't got books at school. We don't got jewelry and cars and any land or money, and when my daddy goes into town, he can't shop in the white stores and has to take off his hat when he passes white folk and say *ma'am* and *sir* to 'em even if they's real young."

"Is it terrible being a black girl?" Beth asked.

Evette looked down at the dirt. "It ain't so bad. It's just you don't ever get things you wants. But my daddy and mama, they say we should be real proud about our place and keep our self-respect. They say that's more important than having. That's what they say."

"Maybe."

We stayed quiet for a little while. Then Evette looked at me and Beth. "What's it like to be white girls?"

I thought about it, but I didn't have any answer. "It's not like anything. It's just the way I am."

"It's true," Beth said.

Evette kicked dirt with her raggy shoes. "That's 'cause y'all don't gotta think about it. You don't gotta know all the time you're a white girl. That's why I don't want no kids, 'cause they'd always know that they's black."

In the Woods Near McPherson's Pond

The next day, after church and Sunday dinner, we drove out and walked my daddy's cotton, corn, and tobacco fields between Clio and Dunbar. Me and Beth and McCall followed along behind Daddy, Mama, and Aunt Greer. Trudging through that hazy and humid white air, McCall said that just the night before he'd made up a list of the top fifty meanest animals on the entire earth. Giving it a scientific going over, he'd decided the number-one meanest was a tossup between wolverines and white sharks. "Wolverines are nasty things. That's a fact. But you wanna know something that's a surprise? The first snake isn't on the list till number twelve. Alligators are. I got 'em at six. Lions and tigers are number three and four and grizzly bears are number five."

Beth said, "I don't even know what a wolverine looks like."

"They ain't so big, like about three feet is all, but they can kill caribou and even a moose, I suppose. They look somewhere's between a raccoon and a bear with the most gigantic claws you ever saw."

Beth looked like she was thinking about what he'd told her. "Are any around here?" she asked.

"Naw. Don't worry. They're up in Canada and the like."

I had a question. "Were any bugs on your list?"

"Darby, bugs ain't mean. They're just annoying."

"How 'bout wolves?"

"Got 'em at twenty-six."

Beth asked, "Did you put crabs on it?"

"They ain't so bad, either. Mostly I got sharks and bears and some of the big cats."

We stopped at one of the slumping houses in my daddy's fields. The six of us sat on the porch in wicker chairs that were unraveling and turning gray. A rabbit ran from a bush, and I told McCall he ought to put one of them on his list of meanest animals.

He ignored me.

Beth told him, "It's neat that you think about that stuff."

"Yeah, it is," he agreed.

When we got back to the truck, we were tired. Daddy drove us over to Hunt's Bluff, where it's always cooler because of the wind. Sitting atop a rise that overlooks the twisty, turny Great Pee Dee River, which is known for its fishing and moonshiners and flooding, we gulped lemonade and ate biscuits that Annie Jane had made. Spread about on a blanket, the five of us listened to Daddy discuss the Civil War and how the Yankee army had made a mess of the area, burning all the homes along the river, even though some of them were the best in South Carolina. It was a terrible, sad affair, he said. I tried to imagine all that smoke and flames, but I couldn't. Not too long after that, me and Beth and McCall piled into Daddy's trunk, and we all headed home with the big ashy sky curving toward the ground and landing like a waterfall on faraway treetops.

✳   ✳   ✳

Mr. Fairchild picked Beth up before supper. She gave me a hug, and when she was gone I didn't have anything to do. Wandering upstairs, I sat on my bed. Thinking I might write another article, I got out some paper, except I didn't have any ideas, good or bad.

At six-thirty, like always, we ate. Afterward, I went

back to my bedroom and looked out into the dark. I thought about Beth and how she and Evette were finally friends. Scooting into my bathroom, I searched out the window and through the trees and across the field. Evette's tenant house had the weakest lantern light coming from inside. It looked like a lonely star in outer space. It reminded me of an anthill that anyone could step on, like it didn't have any chance. I went back to my bed and picked up some paper and sewed out another newspaper notebook. When I was done, I took my pencil and started writing.

Later, after I had finished my story, Mama came in to make sure I was ready for bed. I asked her if our great-granddaddy had owned any slaves.

With her eyes sparkling, she said, "Before I answer that, we gotta skin the cat."

Raising my arms, she yanked off my dirty shirt, which is what she meant by "skin the cat." While I slid on my nightgown, Mama said, "Neither of your great-granddaddies ever did. Nobody in our family owned any property before the war. But the fact of the matter is that everybody working a farm had them. It was just the way. A person didn't even think about it. They lived from the land, and to do that they needed help. There wasn't any sort of hate or anger involved, which is what everyone seems to have forgotten."

I asked, "For setting slaves free, was the Civil War kinda a good thing?"

Mama straightened like I'd slapped one of her legs. "Now, don't ever think that, Darby. Don't you ever. We lost some of our kin in that war. All the families around here lost somebody. The South would be all the better if those boys had lived. I'm not saying things shouldn't have changed. I'm not saying that it was right for people to have slaves, but don't ever think the war was a good thing. That's wrong."

I said, "Yes, ma'am."

✳   ✳   ✳

The next day, I got home from the Murchison School and fetched my story. Tucking it under an arm, I ran down the rows to wait for Evette. Sitting myself between cotton plants, I looked back at Ellan, the chicken house, the Grab, and all those outbuildings. They wavered in the heat and blowing dust. As poor as we sometimes seemed, my family owned a nice home, and we made do. Mama sold milk and dairy at the Douglas and Johns grocery store in Bennettsville. After Thanksgiving, she'd get me and some sharecropper kids to collect pecans from out of our trees, which she'd sell to a man before

Christmas. That's why, every year, we got Christmas presents. It's on account of pecans and hard work. But poor Evette, her family didn't have those extras. They picked in the fields for my daddy and went mostly without.

Leaning down, I spotted the tiny, curled body of a dead boll weevil, the wormy insect that ruins cotton plants. Taking a toe, I smashed it into the dirt so that it disappeared. Even though Daddy gives me a nickel for every jar of boll weevils I pick, I still hate those things.

Hearing voices, I raised my eyes and saw Evette and her brothers halfway down the dirt lane to their house. I got up and met them. "Hey, Joebean and Lucius," I told them.

"Hey, Darby," they said.

Evette pointed at the notebook I had. "You got another story writ up?"

Nodding, I said, "You wanna edit it?"

"Long as my name gets in the paper again."

"It's gonna," I promised.

I sat outside while Evette changed into her play clothes. Then we went through the field and into the woods. Sitting down on top of a log, she read what I'd done. She read it again, and, lifting her face real slow, she gave me a look.

"Is it okay?" I asked.

"Just needs some smoothing out. This one's done more professional than the last." She smiled at me.

"Do you think it's good?"

"I do," she told me, taking my pencil and marking my newspaper article in what seemed like a hundred different spots. She saw me watching, and said, "It ain't nothing."

We worked together for a long while, till dark was coming fast. Then we closed up my notebook and ran out from under all those trees. Stopping at Evette's yard, I said, "Beth likes you now."

"I likes her, too," Evette told me.

Through the ratty screen door of her house, her daddy stuck his head out. "You best get in here, Evette," he called. "Hey, Miss Carmichael," he said to me.

"Hey, Elwood," I called back.

Running toward Ellan, I went through the back door and slumped against a wall to read my article beneath an electric light.

✳   ✳   ✳

In the morning, while we were eating breakfast, somebody knocked at our back door. Annie Jane went down,

153

and a few minutes later she escorted a black man up to the kitchen. He was tall and strong-seeming.

He told us all, "Morning ma'ams and sirs. I'm sorry to interrupt your breakfast."

Daddy stood. "Jerome, what can I help you with?"

Jerome didn't meet my daddy in the eye. He looked awkward, and after a moment I recognized that he was the man from Beth's daddy's office, the man whose boy had been killed.

"Are you okay?" Daddy asked him.

Nodding, the man kept his pupils glued to his crackled boots. "Sir, I am okay, except . . . well . . . I got myself another situation, is all."

"Go on," Daddy said.

"All right, Mr. Carmichael. Yes, all right. I'm gonna say 'cause my new problem is my family. We been kicked offa Mr. Dunn's property, and he says if we come back or makes more trouble round Marlboro County, we gonna get ourselves kilt."

Daddy stared at him before asking, "When did this happen?"

"Two nights back, sir. We been staying off in the woods near McPherson's Pond, but we can't do that forever. See, I didn't wanna come here."

"It's all right," my daddy told him.

"It's just we got nowheres to go. We don't got

154

nothin', really."

Daddy said, "Do you have family somewhere?"

"Up in Fayetteville, sir. They's the closest. I got me a sister'd take us in."

Daddy studied the air in front of him. "Well, we gotta get you up to Fayetteville. You can't stay around these parts anymore. I'm sorry."

"That's . . . that's okay, sir. I knows it myself."

Mama frowned at my daddy. "Sherman, what are you thinking?" She stared at him. "You can't take them up to Fayetteville, not with all that's been happening. You need to mind your own business is what you need. You need to think about this family and our place in the community."

For the first time I can remember, though, Daddy ignored Mama. Looking over at McCall, he asked, "You think you can run the store this morning?"

McCall told him, "I can do it, yeah."

"All you gotta do is take notes as to who's buying what. This time a year we rarely have people pay cash."

"Yes, sir," McCall said.

Standing, Mama threw down her napkin and marched out of the kitchen.

Daddy said, "McCall, if anyone asks, you tell them I'm up in Laurinburg for the morning. You say I'll be back this afternoon."

"I don't gotta go to school when you return, do I?"

Daddy said, "I suppose not, McCall. You get the day off."

"Can I help?" I asked, wanting the day off, too.

Daddy nodded. "Darby, sweetie, you can help by not saying anything to anyone about this. Nothing. You just go on to school like normal. Okay?"

"Yes, sir," I said, feeling low, like I didn't have a real mission.

Daddy asked Jerome, "Do you have a lot of belongings with you?"

Jerome shook his head. "Near 'bouts nothing, sir. We don't got nothin' 'cause Mr. Dunn didn't give us no time to collect stuff. We grabbed up a few things, two pictures of Devin and some clothes."

"Jerome," Daddy said, "I'm sorry. I really am. But we have to get y'all out of here. That's what's important right now."

❋   ❋   ❋

During school, I imagined my daddy's car sputtering north, past Laurinburg and up toward North Carolina. I imagined Jerome and his wife and daughter scrunched flat down in the back seat so that no one would see them. I could picture the blue sky, and I saw the sun gleaming on the car's hood and my daddy talking to the Hawkins family as they went, as mosquito hawks flew up around the windows and bright red songbirds swooped over the fields. It's such a pretty drive, it didn't seem like anything bad could happen to anyone between Bennettsville and North Carolina. Then, before lunch, a terrible picture came into my head. The Ku Klux Klan men stopped Daddy's car. Jumping out, they set off their shotguns into Daddy and the Hawkins family. I nearly screamed out loud.

Miss Burstin stopped what she was doing and asked me if I was feeling okay.

"Yes, ma'am," I answered her with a catch in my throat.

"You look pale."

"I'm okay, ma'am."

At lunch break, I trod slowly down the Murchison School's steps. As I walked across the pretty front lawn, doodlebugs scurried in the dirt when my feet came down. I went on down the street and arrived at Mr. Salter's office, where I shoved the door open and stepped in. Then I got out my newspaper notebook, which was already unraveling because I hadn't made it as good as the first one.

"Well, hello, Darby," Mr. Salter called from behind

his desk.

"Hey, Mr. Salter," I answered.

He ducked his head to get a better sight of my face. "You okay?"

"Yes, sir."

"You got another story for me?"

"Yes, sir."

"Well, that's exciting," he declared. Tilting back in his chair, he told me, "Everyone loved the piece about your uncle. I had so many compliments I stopped keeping count. I hope people told you."

"People said nice things," I promised him.

"It was a great story," he said. "Readers like what you have to say and the way you say it."

"That's real good, sir," I said.

Untilting in his chair, Mr. Salter leaned forward. He wiped an inky hand through his dark hair. "Darby, is something wrong?"

I said, "No, sir." I lifted up my newspaper notebook for him. "You think you might wanna put this story in the paper, too?"

Taking it, he said, "If I didn't, the whole town would tar and feather me." Relaxed, he cracked open my notebook and looked over my newest column. It started by saying how surprised I was to hear that black people up North lived in nice neighborhoods and that some owned things like houses and cars. Then I told how I thought it was strange because I'd never seen such a thing. But it was true, and it seemed funny to me that it could be that way somewhere else but not in Marlboro County. To me, it proved that people want nearly the same thing in the world. They want to own nice stuff and live in a nice way. I also said it was sad how the oldest black men have to take their hats off when they talk to white folks, no matter how young, which doesn't make any sense and must be awfully embarrassing on top of that.

I wrote how things should be done more evenly, and that everybody ought to get respect for being friendly instead of being white or black. I finished the newspaper column by saying that nobody wants to live knowing that things won't ever be nice, and I hoped that one day a black tenant farmer would roar through town in the prettiest Cadillac ever, and maybe if a white man needed a ride home, he'd give him one.

When Mr. Salter was finished, his throat made a funny clicking sound. With his mouth flat and bothered-looking, he said, "This is very different from the other two. It's got its flaws and all, but . . . it's good. It's just inflammatory. You know what that means?"

"No, sir."

"It means it's rabble-rousing, that it could cause

some folks to react in an angry fashion, which is, in some cases, perfect. There's a whole school of journalism that's devoted to stirring up trouble. It's called muckraking, and it's helped change a lot of people's feelings about issues. The thing is . . . Marlboro County is already jumpy and unstable because of what happened out at Turpin Dunn's place. We got some folks who feel a crime was committed, and others that don't see anything wrong, and they're at each other's throats." Mr. Salter toppled his head back and looked straight at the ceiling like it might give him an idea. "See what I mean?"

Disappointed, I asked, "You're worried about your windows getting broken?"

"My windows, my business, and my family. If I print something like this, some people might say I got strange political leanings or that I'm not patriotic or something. I don't know. It could cause me some real trouble."

Mr. Salter's body sagged. "Darby, sweetie, your writing is a gift. I hope you recognize that. You're gonna have a lot of years to hash out these sorts of issues. You're good. I promise. But I can't run this type of story. I just can't."

I looked away. My heart was pounding in my chest.

"I'm sorry," he said.

But that didn't make me feel better. It didn't make sense. Why couldn't he put a small column about blacks in his paper without worrying? It was no wonder I hadn't ever heard of black people owning houses and cars. Nobody could write anything good about them. "Can . . . can I have my notebook back?"

Mr. Salter weighed it in his hands, then put it on his desk. He put up a finger and reached into a drawer. Rummaging around, he found three professional note-pads, which he gave me.

Holding them, so perfect and clean, I wanted to smile but I couldn't.

He said, "I'm giving you those so that you'll keep writing. Okay? You should. You got a good conscience and a kind personality. I don't want the fact that I'm not taking this story to discourage you."

Flipping through the blank pages, I said flatly, "These even got lines to write on."

"Yeah, they do."

"They're nice."

Lifting my head, I asked again, "Mr. Salter, since you don't want it, can I also have my story back?"

"Oh, yeah, Darby. Sure." He laughed. "It's . . . it's just that I don't wanna let it go. It's good. I mean, I kind of see this as a lesson in humanity from the mouth of a child."

"What do you mean?" I asked him.

He chuckled and told me, "I'm just spouting third-rate philosophy."

Confused, I said, "So can I have it back, sir?"

Taking a deep breath, he handed me my story. "Write something else," he said. "You write some more. People like your column."

"I'm gonna write something, maybe tonight."

Mr. Salter took his hands and massaged his face. "Now, Darby, I'm as guilty as everyone else."

"What do you mean, Mr. Salter?" I asked, but I sort of understood.

Balling up a fist, he thumped it on his desk. "Never mind."

✳ ✳ ✳

That afternoon, I searched out the school windows so that I might spot my daddy's Buick go by on the street. There are about ten different routes into town, though, so I knew he could come back another way. Still, I had to look. Even during our spelling test, I watched the road and couldn't concentrate. I knew I was misspelling nearly every word, but I couldn't help it.

Miss Burstin came over and kneeled beside my

chair. "Darby, are you feeling okay?" she whispered.

"Almost, ma'am," I told her.

"You look out of sorts, child, and you skipped lunch earlier."

Swallowing, I told her, "I went to see Mr. Salter about a new story, is why I didn't eat."

She nodded. "That's wonderful. I'm glad you enjoy writing, but a growing girl needs nourishment."

"I guess," I said, suddenly starving. "He didn't want it anyway," I told her. After saying that, I nearly started to cry. My stomach felt knotted up like a croaker sack.

Miss Burstin gave me a hug. She said, "Sweetheart, if you're going to make a career of writing, you're going to have to get used to rejection. But it hurts. It stings."

I pointed at the test paper in front of me. "For some reason, I can't think."

She nodded. "Why don't you retake the test tomorrow. How about that?"

I answered, "Thank you, Miss Burstin. That'd be better."

"Good," she whispered, and stood. Walking up to her desk, she fetched something from a drawer and came back and put five saltines beside my paper. Clapping her hands, she called out, "Five minutes! Don't forget, *i* before *e* except after *c*. It's a rule."

At the end of the school day, I said goodbye to Beth,

who begged me to go home with her. When I told her I couldn't, she said, "Please, please, please!" But I lied and said that my daddy had given me an instruction, and I couldn't get out of it. So I wandered up the street to the Carmichael Block. Off in the distance, a barrier of clouds looked like giant bales of unwashed cotton. They seemed stacked up toward the top of the sky, heavy and solid with dirty white tops and undersides. For some reason, they made the sunlight extra yellow.

Anxious, I went slowly down Main Street. When I got to Carmichael Dry Goods, I waited and waited till I got up my nerve. Then I turned and pushed through the front door.

Daddy was there, talking to Mr. Salter and leaning against the counter.

"Hey, Daddy! I can't believe you got back already!"

"Hey, Darby. Yeah, I did. I returned a while ago."

Mr. Salter said, "Hello there, Darby."

Relieved that my daddy was back, I didn't feel so bad about my story. I said, "Hello, sir."

"You look happy," Daddy said.

I told him, "I'm just glad about stuff, is all." I wanted so bad for him to pick me up like I was a little kid, but I knew he wouldn't. Slipping my books alongside his elbow, I patted one of his hands.

Mr. Salter said, "Darby, you know what me and

your daddy were discussing?"

"What, sir?"

"Your daddy and I have been talking about your new story. Matter of fact, that's why I'm here. He thought you'd be going home with Beth, but I guess he was wrong, which is fortunate for me because I'd like to show him your article. Do you mind? What I told him is, if he approves, I'm gonna run it tomorrow."

I stared at him for a second. "Really?" I shouted.

"Yes, Darby, if he approves."

"Do you, Daddy?" I asked.

"First I have to read it."

Diving for my books, I pulled out my newspaper notebook and gave it to him. "It's the first thing," I said.

Flipping it open, Daddy looked at me, cleared his throat, and read. Scowling the entire way, he didn't seem to like it much.

When he was done, I stared at him.

Daddy scratched his chin. Placing my story on the counter, he took a long draw of wind, and said, "I like it. It's strong and thoughtful, especially for a nine-year-old. The thing is, I was hoping we wouldn't have to think more about this sort of thing for a while. Big Darby absolutely hates the way Marlboro County seems so rancorous and divided these days." He flicked a wad of dust off the side of the cash register.

Mr. Salter said, "Sherman, that's why I wanted you to see it."

Daddy said, "In a way, I wish you'd run it without asking me. I suppose I'm as chicken as the next guy."

My mouth flopped open. "You are not, Daddy."

Daddy glanced at Mr. Salter, then down at me. "Heck, Darby, if this got run, it would upset your mama something awful, that's for sure. She'd be real upset. Not that she sides with the Klan, she just hates things being stirred up." He scratched his chin again and considered. "Funny, I wish it wasn't so, but as it stands, my best judgment says this should be in the paper. It's a real eye opener when a child sees things more clearly than adults. It really is."

"That's what I thought," Mr. Salter told him.

"Go on and run it," Daddy instructed.

"You're sure, Sherman?"

Daddy thought for a second more. "I am," he stated.

Jumping into the air, I shouted, "This is the best day of my whole life!"

Mr. Salter smiled. He said, "She's a little muckraker, Sherman. You better watch yourself."

Daddy laughed. "Heck, I can handle it. I'm used to it. Both my kids are attracted to trouble."

* * *

Not so long after that, when Mr. Salter was gone and
my daddy was waiting on a customer, I heard a familiar
sound outside. Tiny hooves clip-clopped on the sidewalk. Happy and daring, I went to the door and looked
out to see Chester roll past with Mercury pulling him in
the goat cart. Yanking the door open, I stepped outside,
and called, "Chester." He kept rolling. "Chester!" I
shouted, and everyone around looked at me.

He stopped.

I caught up and put my hand on Mercury's nose. I
said, "Chester?"

"Yeah?" he answered shyly.

"Chester, I wanna ride with Mercury sometimes.
Like before."

He nodded.

Brave from happiness, I said, "I know you got a
crush on me, but I don't mind. I just wanna ride. I don't
mind that you got a crush."

Peeking up at me, he said, "You don't?"

"It's sorta nice," I said.

"You . . . think?"

"Yeah," I said. Then, glancing all around to see if
anyone was looking, I stepped close and gave him a
quick hug. I don't even know why I did it. Mama would

have killed me forever if she heard about it. "See. We're friends. It doesn't matter about that other stuff."

Smiling and red, Chester stuttered, "You . . . you wanna ride right now?"

"I gotta go help my daddy. Maybe I can ride tomorrow?"

He said. "I . . . sorta missed not talking to you."

"Same here," I said back, smiling.

Two Storms

That was the night of the storm, when all the farmers in Marlboro County lost at least one shed and Crooked Creek rose up and flooded the Gulf, where most of the black-owned shops in Bennettsville are built. It was the night a bunch of tornadoes twisted across the fields, and a farmer named Mr. MacKnight thought he'd lost all of his mules in a barn near Tatum. It was the night that a gigantic tree fell on one of the best homes in town and about ten tenant houses crumbled in. It was an awful, awful storm, and Daddy and me drove home just as it was kicking up.

Watching the thunderhead clouds climbing higher and higher into the sky, all the shopkeepers, including Daddy, closed their stores early. Nervous, me and

Daddy got into the Buick and clanked across town toward Ellan. Just about halfway home, the wind started gusting. Then sheets and sheets of rain drummed the ground so that you could hardly see. Daddy drove as fast as he could, but branches were cartwheeling into the roadway, making him weave like a chased chicken. Out on the open highway, as we raced between fields of cotton, it was nearly as pitch-dark as midnight. Then lightning began crackling and combing the fields and trees, giving everything a gleaming whiteness. After ten minutes, we turned onto Ellan's drive and banged down the muddy path to the back of the house. The car barn's doors were swinging wildly back and forth, but Daddy didn't even slow. He drove right in between them just as one caught in a gust, crashing closed behind us.

"I got to get the doors locked before they blow off," Daddy called to me, and I got out and we struggled and wrastled the one closed while the rain stung our cheeks. Then, in a hail of blowing camellia blooms and hard-as-stone pecans, we ran toward the house. At the back door, Daddy shoved me inside, and called, "I need to go check the cows." Then his big body disappeared into the gray, sideways rain.

Rushing upstairs, I heard someone screaming and crying, and in the kitchen I found Mama holding tight to Aunt Greer, whose eyes were as big as bottle tops. Over my aunt's howls, Mama yelled for me to help McCall and Annie Jane shut the upstairs windows.

I raced into the hallway and jumped up the steps. Halfway to the top, something crashed in the parlor, bringing me to a stop. Confused, I turned and skittered back down the stairs. I was near the bottom when the lights shut off, and in the sudden darkness, I missed a step and found myself rolling and bouncing into the foyer. Getting up, I chased into the parlor, where I could see that the window was poked through with a busted tree limb.

As the curtains blew as crazy as a ghost, the rain swished in and was getting everything wet. Scared, I gathered in the slippery-as-an-eel drapes and tried to keep the rain from soaking the floor. On the roadway out front, lightning fireballs sizzled. Thunder shook Ellan. A few minutes passed that way, and McCall and Annie Jane came rushing down the steps. Together, we gathered the twisty, fluttering drapes and pushed the limb out the window.

"Where's Daddy?" McCall shouted in my ear.

"He's gone out to the dairy barn," I yelled back.

"Lawd, Lawd, Lawd," Annie Jane was saying.

The storm licked and growled over the top of us, but we blocked the rain good, even when it turned to hail. Pushing hard, we held the heavy curtains flat against the wall. Then the wind gave out the nastiest of gusts and snapped the thick curtain rod, sending the drapes spinning and flopping down on top of Annie Jane's head. Stumbling and bleeding a little, she grabbed up a blanket and helped us hold that into place.

Shortly, Daddy was alongside us and taking over. He directed Annie Jane to sit, and we watched her fall into a chair. By himself, Daddy held that blanket in place, so that I was all the sudden so tired I began to shiver. Stumbling backward on the slick floor, one of my arms began to throb something awful. It went *bonk, bonk, bonk,* and my eyes watered. Then my teeth started clicking, and that *click-click-click* sound filled my ears.

The storm lasted only about an hour, but when it was over the air was thin and freezing cold so that you could see steam when you breathed. Then the prettiest thing happened. Way on the horizon, the clouds scattered like the shreds of Evette's dresses, and the last rays of daylight shot into the house. Like a hot dot in the cold air, the top part of the yellow sun fell into the bare trees. I held my achy arm and began to cry.

Dropping the drenched blanket out the window, Daddy checked on Annie Jane. He put a thumb against the bump on her head. "You got it pretty good, huh?" he said.

"It ain't nothing, Mr. Carmichael, but a good knot and a scratch."

"You sure?"

"Yes, sir, Mr. Carmichael. You go on and mind Darby," she instructed.

Directly, Daddy turned and came over to me. "Darby, sweetheart, you okay?"

"Daddy," I sniffled, "my arm . . . it hurts to high heaven."

Daddy gently lifted my throbbing wrist and gave it a good inspection.

I grunted in pain.

Daddy whispered, "Darby, sweetie, you did something to it, that's for sure." He touched around a swelled-up area.

Whimpering, I said, "I tumbled down the steps is how. That's how I did it, I guess."

✳   ✳   ✳

It turned out a lot of people got it worse than me during the storm, but being that my daddy is considered a real important person, an hour later Dr. McNeil came out to Ellan and wrapped my arm with a long, narrow strip of cotton. With his glasses hanging on the tip of his nose, he told me it wasn't a break but a sprain and that I'd be feeling better so quick it wasn't worth me going to his office. From out of his doctor's bag, he found a clear bottle of medicine. "You drink a tablespoon of this before bed," he instructed. But that stuff tasted so bad I couldn't even stand to smell it. I'd have rather hurt all over than swallow a tiny thimbleful.

Marlboro County was a mess. Things were flooded and trees were all the sudden bare, their colorful November leaves torn off in the wind. At Ellan, two shutters had been ripped and tossed into the backyard, and a whole row of shingles had cracked and slid off the roof. Plus, Daddy said that the window in our parlor was ruined. On the ground, tree limbs were scattered, and all of the flowers on my daddy's camellia bushes had been blown clean off. Worse, my mama's pecans were littered across the yard and down past the dairy barn. It took us days to gather them up.

All over, people had stories, the best being old Mr. MacKnight's. He says that after the storm passed, he went about checking his outbuildings, and when he got to where his mule barn was supposed to be, the whole thing was missing. Scared, he looked everywhere for it. At daybreak, he says he rose and drove the fields around his house, looking and looking. Finally, just as he was giving up, he spotted the barn way down a dirt lane in the middle of a cornfield. When he reached it, he said that the outside looked fine, like nothing at all had happened. Excited, he flung open the barn doors . . . and there were all his mules, happy as can be after getting picked up and carried for almost half a mile. He says he was so relieved that he trembled like the biggest baby you ever saw.

Daddy told me that people don't believe Mr. MacKnight's story. A man who should know says that the barn always was right there and that Mr. MacKnight was getting too old and lonely to remember where his own outhouse was. Still, I believe him. I believe that a tornado could've done that sort of thing, because if one did, it means there's a small amount of magic in the world.

The morning after the storm, the front page of the Bennettsville Times announced, "Massive Front Brings Storms and Tornadoes." A smaller headline explained, "Tree Falls on One of Bennettsville's Finest Homes and the Gulf Floods." The whole top portion of the front page was filled with that stuff. It even had a picture of a tornado in a cotton field. Still, there was plenty of room left for other articles. Underneath the top half of the paper, there was a story about the price of cotton falling and falling and another that told how a dog in

Brownsville could bark "The Star-Spangled Banner" nearly perfect. At the very bottom, in a box, Mr. Salter had run my column. Above it, he'd written in medium-sized letters, "The Enlightened Views of a Child." In smaller words was written, "Another article by Marlboro County's favorite columnist, Little Darby Carmichael, with editorial assistance from Evette."

My daddy calls my article the second big storm in as many days, but I don't exactly agree; my story didn't push over trees or knock down houses. It didn't do what the cold front did.

The funny thing is, when I went to school in the morning, I didn't even remember that my newspaper article was coming out. All I could think about was the storm and tumbling down the steps. I was telling everyone about that. I said, "Then the lights went out, and I nearly flew through the air, bashing my arm on the floor." When Principal Casper requested my company halfway through arithmetic, I had no idea what he wanted. Shuffling down the hall, I figured he was mad at me for calling an older girl "dumb as dirt" the day before.

Closing his office door, Principal Casper didn't say a word, not right off. He sat down behind his desk and stared at me.

"Yes, sir?" I asked him, nervous.

He fanned a hand above the newspaper on his desk. When I saw my article, I spouted, "It came out!"

Cracking his knuckles, he growled, "Yes, it did." His eyes flared. "You do realize that this is going to cause a certain amount of uproar? You do realize that?"

I was so surprised, I couldn't move or speak.

"It's the kind of thing a lot of parents aren't going to like. It's the kind of thing some of your friends might not like, either. This story could make you very unpopular."

I whispered, "Saying the truth is what newspaper girls do."

"Maybe and maybe not, Miss Carmichael. Listen, I won't beat around the bush here." He leaned forward so that all I could see was his big head. "I'm glad you enjoy writing for the newspaper, but I don't ever want you doing something like this again. I don't need this kind of headache. You hear?"

"Yes, sir."

"After church on Sunday, I'll talk to your parents about this, too. Now, please, Miss Carmichael, return to your class."

Worried, I scuffed down the fancy hallway and up the steps and scooted back into my desk alongside Beth, who I smiled at. I looked around the room at my friends and the Lint Heads from the Mill Village, and I wondered which of them would hate me now. I wished I'd kept my big trap shut and that Mr. Salter hadn't put my column in his paper.

Before leaving for lunch, Beth asked, "What did Principal Casper want?"

Staring at the floor, I answered, "To talk about my newspaper column."

She said, "That's all?"

"Yeah."

"I was worried you were in trouble."

"I wasn't," I told her.

She said, "See you after lunch."

"See ya."

While classmates left for home, I fetched my coat, and while I was yanking it on, Miss Burstin walked over and put her arm around my shoulders. "Darby, dear, I'd like you to walk with me to lunch, okay? I feel like I should say a few things."

Uneasy, I answered, "Yes, ma'am."

Once everyone was gone, me and Miss Burstin went down the steps and out onto the front walk. Underneath a bare tree, she stopped, and said, "You told me that Mr. Salter wasn't interested in your latest story."

I twisted and looked at her. "He . . . he wasn't till he thought about it. After he did, he decided that he should put it in his paper."

She nodded. "Darby, sweetheart, I'm sure you know that you've upset some people. Some are going to be very unhappy about the subject of your column."

"Yes, ma'am," I answered.

"Still," she said, "I want you to know how exceptionally proud of you I am. I really am."

Taken aback, I smiled weakly. "You are?"

"It was a very heartfelt piece of writing," she explained as she started walking again, her pretty shoes making a hollow sound on the leaf-covered cement.

I asked, "Miss Burstin, what's *heartfelt* mean?"

"It means it was genuine, from the heart," she told me as we approached the house where all the teachers live and eat their meals.

"Miss Burstin, what's *enlightened* mean?"

"As in the name of your column?"

"Yes, ma'am. Mr. Salter named my article. That's why I don't know the word."

"It means intelligent. When Mr. Salter wrote 'The Enlightened Views of a Child,' he was trying to say that you see this particular issue more clearly than many adults."

"Does he think I'm smarter than some adults?"

"Maybe," she answered.

"You think I am?"

"Possibly," she told me, chuckling.

Feeling better, I laughed, too. "Do you think some of the class is gonna hate me?"

Stepping from a curb, Miss Burstin said, "No, because I won't tolerate that kind of behavior."

At lunch, we got seated and said our prayers and passed the food. The teachers and farm kids around me ate so quietly you could hear their spoons and forks scraping across the plates or spearing pieces of meat. It was awful. After lunch was over, Miss Burstin walked with me back to the Murchison School, and I said, "No one even admitted they read my story."

"Some will, Darby, and some won't," she said.

✳   ✳   ✳

When school was done, I decided to stay in town with Beth. I didn't really want to see Evette just yet. I jammed my books beneath my good arm, and we left the Murchison School. Hopping down the front steps one at a time, we laughed. It felt like our legs were roped together. Cutting catty-corner across the school's front field, we started toward Beth's house. Below our feet, leaves and twigs were as thick as a rug. Walking along, kicking through their floppy wetness, I felt strange and didn't know if I was sad or happy. I didn't know if I wanted people to be mad about my story or if I wanted them to like it.

"You're not listening," Beth notified me.

"Sorry," I told her. "What did you say?"

"I . . . I asked what McCall's favorite color is. Do you know?"

"Naw. Why are you wondering?"

"Just to talk," she told me. "I don't care."

"Maybe he likes brown."

"Well, do you think he likes pink a little?"

"He might," I said.

We kept going, and a man working in a yard stopped his raking and glowered, as mean as a crow, at me. Putting a cigarette to his mouth, he drew in and held the smoke in his chest for a second. Then he let it trickle out from around his tongue. Taking the cigarette and pointing the back part toward us, he said, "You should oughta stick to writing about toads, Darby Carmichael."

Fearful that the man was going to do something terrible, me and Beth started running as fast as we could. I practically flew down that skinny street with all its sweet-seeming places and shortish trees. It was strange, because that part of Bennettsville had never before seemed like a creepy place.

When I finally stopped, Beth caught up and gave

me one of my books.

"I didn't even know I dropped it," I told her, huffing for air.

"I saw it squirt out," she said, huffing too.

Looking back, I watched the mean man rake his yard.

Beth said, "During lunch, Daddy and Mama told me your new story's real brave and smart."

I told her, "Principal Casper said that some people might not like me anymore because of it. He said that my column might make me real unpopular at school."

Walking beside me, Beth all of a sudden laughed. "You know what? It doesn't matter, because I think he's got the biggest head I've ever seen."

I snickered when she said that. "It reminds me of one of those dogs who saves people in the mountains."

She said, "You mean a St. Bernard."

"Yeah."

Beth bounced up and down on her toes, making her dress jump at her knees. "Well, if people still like Principal Casper, they're still gonna like you, 'cause your head is normal size."

With my thumb, I pointed behind us. "Wasn't that man back there stupid?"

Beth declared, "He's an egg-sucking dog."

It took me a second to realize that Beth had said something nasty. Feeling better, I yelped, "Yeah." Then I barked and made a slurping sound.

"Egg-sucking dog!" Beth hollered without looking back.

✳   ✳   ✳

At Beth's house, the cook cut us large hunks of corn bread and put butter on top. Together, we went outside to her daddy's driveway and drew up hopscotch squares with chalk. Finding rocks, we tossed them into our long, long hopscotch arrangement, then started jumping. For some reason, I've always been better than Beth. I can do hopscotch perfect almost every time, including when I'm wearing a thick coat and have an achy wrist.

We fooled around for a long while, but we didn't keep a score.

Late in the afternoon, Chester came home from somewhere. Stopping at the back door, he turned stiffly and gave me a quick wave.

I raised my hand, telling Beth, "He waved."

"He's really dumb," she said.

"Why?"

"'Cause he got in trouble yesterday and has to stay after school all week."

"Maybe it wasn't his fault."

"I bet it was," she declared, pitching her rock onto our hopscotch course.

Shortly, Chester came outside. He toddled toward us, keeping his head tilted sideways, like there was something messed-up about his neck. He stopped by our chalk boxes, and, as soft as can be, he asked if me and Beth wanted to ride on his goat cart.

"Yeah," I said, thinking about how I'd hugged him the afternoon before.

"I'll go get it," he said, like we were forcing him.

We went on playing hopscotch until Chester and Mercury clip-clopped over from the barn. Getting into the cart, me and Beth sat alongside each other. "This is nice to do," I told Chester.

"I reckon," he agreed. "Where do you wanna go?"

"Into town, I guess," Beth said.

"Yeah," I agreed.

Flicking the reins, Chester got Mercury moving along, and we rattled down the drive and out onto the street. Rolling slow, I wished I had a fancy goat cart out at Ellan. But I knew one wouldn't be any good there. It wouldn't be able to get through the mud and ruts of our dirt lane.

On Main Street, we wiggle-wobbled past the Auto Fountain and the A&P. Cars and horse wagons jumbled past us, moving a whole lot quicker. As we waited to cross South Parsonage Street, on the opposite sidewalk, a waitress from the Sanitary Café waved at us.

I waved back.

A minute or so later, a man who is a regular in my daddy's store said, "Well, if it ain't Marlboro County's favorite columnist."

I smiled.

Farther down, on the Carmichael Block, a man who stacks boxes at the Lewis & Breeden drugstore said, "Hello, Little Darby."

"Hey, sir," I said.

Chester gave Mercury's reins a yank, which stopped the goat cold. Twisting about, he asked, "Why's everyone acting so different?"

"I think it's on account of my newspaper story."

Burning

When Daddy and me got home that Wednesday night, Mama was as hot as a firecracker. As we pulled into the car barn, she rushed out the back door of Ellan. By the time Daddy cut off the engine and got from the car, Mama was standing directly in front of him, breathing hard from running. Face knotty with anger, she shook a finger like it was a stick. "Sherman Carmichael, I'll have you know that the telephone started ringing at ten in the morning. Friends of ours, people I've known since the day I came here to teach, were calling to ask what we were thinking. It rang all morning, and they all had the same question, What were we thinking?"

With her eyes narrowed, Mama leaned toward Daddy, and demanded, "What was going on in your head? You tell me, because I surely don't have any idea. How could you let our daughter put that kind of rabble-rousing, that sort of writing in the paper? Do you want to start another controversy in this county? Is that what you want? Because that's what people are asking."

I blabbered, "Mama?"

Swinging about, she glowered at me like one of McCall's wolverines. "Darby, don't say a word, because right now I have a mind to keep you from ever seeing your friend Evette again. Do you hear me?"

Daddy said, "If we're going to argue, we should do it in private."

"I don't want to do it in private, Sherm! I want Darby to see what she has done to this family."

"What's that going to do?"

"It's going to teach her."

"It won't," Daddy declared. "It won't at all, because I was the one who made the decision to run the article. I made the choice, and I'll stand up for it."

Mama said, "I'm sure you will."

"That's right, I'm going to. Because it's important that something like this gets said. Besides, this isn't about blacks exactly. It's about being humane. That's all."

Mama said, "Living here is not about being humane. It's about watching out for your family, making sure you provide."

Daddy told her, "We're going to be fine, Darby. We've got resources. We've got land and the store."

Shaking her head, Mama slowly leaned and fell against Daddy, who hugged her softly. "You should've told me this story was going to come out," she hissed.

"Maybe," he agreed. "But I didn't, and I'm sorry."

Mama started crying. I could see the tears rolling down her cheeks. "It's just that I keep remembering that you two were already threatened once . . . and . . ."

"And we'll probably get threatened again," Daddy told her. "As long as it's threats."

She said, "I . . . I don't understand why you're act-ing this way, Sherman. I don't. You never even used to think about this sort of thing before."

Daddy said, "I did. I always have known what's right and what's wrong. I just never saw a boy beaten to death for stealing a chicken. It pushed me."

Mama didn't speak. Instead, she continued crying on Daddy's shoulder, making me real uncomfortable. Already I was tired from the strange way people had treated me all day, and seeing Mama like that made me near about exhausted.

The three of us walked especially slow toward Ellan's back door. Mama and Daddy were in front of me, their arms around each other. I followed a few steps behind. Looking about the chilly, leaf-covered backyard,

I was glad that we were all alone out in Marlboro County, that we didn't have someone living close enough to ask me how I could be so stupid as to write about blacks.

*   *   *

After dinner, I sat upstairs in my room. It was dark out, and I was scrunched in a chair by the window. For some reason, I could smell the ground outside like it was fresh-tilled even though that was months away. Smelling it got me to wishing it was spring and that summer was around the corner. I wanted to go swimming or fishing with Daddy down at McPherson's Pond. I wanted to forget how things were going. Downstairs, I could hear McCall talking to Mama and Aunt Greer. He was explaining birds to them, how they have different types of feathers. He said, "And they got a fuzzy-type feather and a sharper kind for their wings. Did you know that?"

I got up and lay on top of my bed. McCall's a weird brother, but the way he thinks is neat. For that reason, I always believed he was smarter than me. Whenever I used to say that to Mama, though, she told me that I wasn't exactly right. She said that different people have

189

brains that are good for different things. She said that my brain was good for something I hadn't found yet. But lying there that night, I wished I had the same specialties as McCall, so that I wouldn't ever write newspaper articles again.

The wind blew and rattled my windows, and I rolled onto my side. I didn't feel like going to school the next day, not when most of the kids might not like me anymore. I wanted to stay home and sit beneath the Marlboro County sky, where it was safe and I could feel lucky again.

I fell asleep while McCall talked downstairs. With my face mashed deep into the pretty quilts Mama had sewn from ripped shirts and dresses, I dreamed that all the tenant houses on our farm began floating like hot air balloons. In my dream, I stood in a cotton field and watched fifty falling-apart homes drift about in the windy sky, heading north toward New York City, where blacks have their own neighborhoods and houses and some even have their own cars. The floating tenant houses disappeared over the horizon, and I looked into the fields they'd left behind and saw that nothing was growing.

*　　*　　*

Later in the night, I woke up to the sound of my daddy yelling and King barking. Feeling woozy, I searched over toward Aunt Greer and saw that she was still asleep. Being that I wasn't thinking clearly, I got up and snuck real slow out of the room and down the long steps to the open front door, where McCall was staring outward as if he were a zombie. Following his eyes, I saw what he was looking at, and all the blood in my body seemed to dry up in my veins and heart. Out on our front lawn, by the highway, a huge cross burned in the blackness. It was yellow with long, licking flames, and my daddy and King stood below it. The flames cast a warm, jumpy glow on the trees and the ground, making my daddy and King look like two devils on a volcano top.

Glancing to the side, I realized that Mama stood silent on the porch. The blaze reflected on her cheeks and arms. As she breathed out, steam rolled from her mouth.

I whispered, "Are you scared, Mama?" because I was. The burning cross was the symbol for the Ku Klux Klan.

At first Mama didn't answer. Then, turning to see me, she said slowly, "No, Darby. They wanted to scare me. They wanted to scare all of us. But in lighting that cross, they didn't push me down. They stood me up."

✳   ✳   ✳

Before school, Sheriff McDonnell drove out from Bennettsville to see what was left of the fiery cross. After studying the scene, taking his hands and combing for stuff in the grass, the sheriff came inside and sat at our kitchen table, where he had himself a glass of milk. Drumming some fingers against the chair he sat on, he told us how earlier in the evening somebody had burned a cross in front of the *Bennettsville Times* office. He said that Mr. Salter was furious. "The Klan's getting active again. That's for sure."

Shaking his head, Daddy asked, "Can't you shut them down?"

"Only when they do something illegal."

"Like burning a cross on private property?"

Sheriff McDonnell took a swallow of milk, and some of it soaked into his bristly mustache. "Yeah, that'd qualify," he said. "Thing is, the Klan don't generally operate in Marlboro County. You'll find most of 'em is outsiders. Plus, it's hard to nab those boys. Each one vouches for the other. One will say the other was somewhere else at the time of a crime. That's infuriating, 'cause I know good and well who's responsible for certain things, but my hands are tied. I gotta work within the confines of the law."

Daddy ate some of his eggs. Blotting his mouth with his napkin, he asked, "Do you think we should be scared?"

Sheriff McDonnell took a deep breath. "Like I told Mr. Fairchild after they tossed a brick through his office window, these boys'll likely continue harassing you till you stop doing whatever it is that's getting them mad. In this case, if Darby were to write her next column on something as innocent as bugs or birds, they'd likely as not forget all about you."

Daddy nodded.

"Then again," Sheriff McDonnell said, "if you back off, they win, and I'd hate to see those cowards win anything."

✳   ✳   ✳

On the way to school, McCall turned the Chevrolet onto a little gravel lane called Haircut Road. Setting the choke, he let the car idle. Peering straight ahead, he gripped the wheel like he was trying to squeeze water out of it.

"What's wrong?" I asked him.

He looked at me in a real serious fashion. "I'm just worried about you going to school today."

"You . . . you think something might happen?"

McCall wiped back his hair. "I don't know."

"You must think that something might or you wouldn't've stopped."

He banged a hand against the steering wheel. "Naw, that's not true. I mean, all I'm saying is, if somebody bothers you, you tell 'em they gotta deal with me. You tell 'em I won't think twice about going after 'em."

I tried not to smile, but I always like it when McCall's nice to me. "If someone's mean, I'll say that."

"When you walk into school," he instructed, "just act like nothing happened. You just be yourself and don't worry 'bout all that's going on. It was a good article, and if people had any sense, they'd see it was good, too."

"Thanks, McCall."

Putting the car in gear, he pulled a U-turn. "Right now we gotta watch out for each other."

A few minutes later, as we rumbled past the *Bennettsville Times* office, into the Murchison School parking lot, I studied its front yard unable to see where the cross had burned. I squinted and then widened my eyes, but I didn't see anything. At school, I got out of the car and said to McCall, "I'll tell you if anyone's mean." Feeling anxious, I went off looking for Beth. Zigzagging through the crowd of kids, I didn't glance up to see if anyone was watching me. But just as I got to the Murchison School's front door, somebody called to me from behind. Frightened, I spun about and saw Sissy.

"Darby," Sissy said, rushing up the steps. "Hey, ah . . . you . . . you think we can talk?"

I told her, "I'm going to see if Beth's upstairs. You wanna come?"

Leaning close to one of my ears, she whispered, "If . . . if you don't mind, I wanna talk private for a minute."

Confused, I said, "All right."

"You think we can go somewhere?"

"I guess," I told her, wondering what she wanted to keep secret. We walked down the hall, made a sneaky swerve, and went through a door and into the back section of the school stage, with its heavy red curtains and fiery lights that were dark on account of the electric being off. Seating ourselves on the edge of the platform, we swung our legs back and forth and looked out at the pretty theater seats that were lined up in rows. Behind them, the fanciest columns held up the balcony.

Because it looked so good, the theater was my favorite room in school.

"Are y'all right?" I asked Sissy. I wanted to hurry up and talk so that I could run upstairs and tell Beth about the burning cross.

Sissy gently clomped her heels against the side of the stage. It took her a bit, but real softly she answered, "I don't know."

"Why's that?"

She raised a shoulder. "Well . . . 'cause by mistake I might've done something bad."

"What?"

Wrangling her hands in her lap, Sissy seemed hypnotized by the spidery way her fingers moved. She said, "I don't wanna say, I don't," she mumbled, "but I gotta. I know I do . . . I mean, it sounds like nothing, but it's not. What I mean is, yesterday my daddy picked me up from school, and the first thing he asked was, 'Sissy, do you know who Darby's friend Evette is?' I didn't think anything of it, so I said she was a black girl on your farm. I said she was at your birthday party and that you had her sit at your special birthday table instead of me. I told him you acted like she was your and Beth's pretend sister and that I said it was impossible on account of her being black. You remember?"

Feeling like I might topple over, I squeaked, "Yeah."

Sissy kept on. "Anyways, when we stopped at our house, he told me I couldn't see you anymore for a while. Just like that, he said you and Evette had written something awful in the *Bennettsville Times*. He said you were mixed up in things that are way over your head and that your daddy and mama must be responsible for giving you such terrible ideas."

I wanted to tell her it wasn't true, but I couldn't say a word, for feeling so awful and shivery. Sissy's daddy had grown up friends with my daddy. I never would've guessed he would tell Sissy she couldn't see me anymore.

Finally, I gurgled, "Sorry, Sissy."

"Why're you saying sorry to me? You didn't do anything bad."

I nodded. "I don't know why I said it."

"The bad thing," said Sissy, "is that my daddy and some of his friends hate the blacks, and I'm worried he might say something mean to your daddy or mama. That's what I thought about after I told him that stuff. After I said it, I wished I hadn't. All night I wished I'd just shut up about Evette 'cause I know your mama and daddy are nice, and I always wanted for you and me and Beth to be best friends. But now you and Beth won't ever want me to come visit."

I said, "Your daddy won't let you anyway."

In a weak voice, Sissy said, "Yeah."

I asked, "Do you think your daddy hates other kindsa people, too?"

Sissy replied, "Like who?"

"Like Indians or French people? People like those?"

"I never heard him say anything."

I said, "It's sorta sad he's that way, isn't it?"

"Yeah," she answered.

A Communist

On the day Sissy told me about her daddy, I skipped lunch and went down to the *Bennettsville Times* office. Slithering through the crowds of kids stomping home to eat, I rushed along Fayetteville Avenue and up the steps to the newspaper office door. Stopping, I built up my nervous guts by searching the grass for charred bits of cross. Then I turned and pushed at the door, which was locked tight. I knocked, and heard some footsteps, then saw Mr. Salter through the glass. He clicked the bolt and pulled the door back.

"Well, if it isn't Darby Carmichael. We've stirred up some trouble, haven't we?"

I dropped my head, wondering if he was mad. "Are you upset?" I asked.

Mr. Salter shook his head. "The last person I'm upset at is you. As a matter of fact, I'm happy I ran your article. What's bothering me are the narrow-minded folks who canceled their subscription to the paper. And of course, it'd be nice if the Klan hadn't burned a cross in front of the building. That would've been nice."

I told him, "Last night we got a cross burned in front of our house, too."

Breathing in deep, Mr. Salter wandered back toward his desk. "I heard about that," he said, "and I'm sorry. I really am."

I followed after him and sat in a chair.

Mr. Salter asked, "How'd you hurt your arm?"

I explained, "I fell down some steps during the storm." Touching the cotton wrap on my wrist, I asked, "Mr. Salter, how many people stopped getting the newspaper?"

He said, "Not enough to bother me, really. Twelve families did it. Twelve families in all of Marlboro County jumped ship. Probably already signed up to get the competition delivered. I won't miss that money. It just shows how strongly some people feel." Putting his hands behind his head, he leaned back in his chair. "Of course, I've gotten a few phone calls from people who aren't happy with me, but that's all right. That's what newspaper writing is about. I don't mind creating a small ruckus."

"You don't?"

"Not so much."

"Okay," I said.

Sitting forward again, he rested his elbows on his desk. "By the way, in case you're worried, I spoke with the sheriff, and he says that a majority of the Klan members aren't from around here. He says the real troublemakers aren't our neighbors or friends. I find a certain comfort in that."

"Yes, sir," I agreed softly. Scooting about on the slick wooden chair, I figured it was a good time to admit to how Sissy had blabbermouthed to her daddy. "Mr. Salter?"

"Yeah, sweetie?"

"I got something to admit."

He tilted his head forward to listen better.

In a single gush, I let it pour from my mouth. "People know who Evette is on account of her coming to my birthday party. A friend of mine told her daddy, and he might've told other people."

Mr. Salter stared at me. Then he laughed. "Well, heck, that's all right. I knew it would eventually happen. It had to. Don't worry about that. Now we can use Evette's last name. What do you think?"

Surprised, it took me a minute to say, "That'd be all right."

"Probably should've done it from the start, huh?"

"Mr. Salter, you know what? I might not ever write another article. I've been thinking on it, and I might quit being a newspaper girl."

He adjusted forward. "Now, wouldn't that be a shame. It'd be a real waste."

"I know," I whispered, "but I might."

"I hope you don't."

"I guess I didn't realize it would be this way."

For a few minutes, we didn't speak a word. Then I said, "Maybe I should go, sir?" Standing up, I turned and started walking.

"Darby?"

At the door, I looked back.

"You be strong, and if you can't be, you let the adults be strong for you. This'll all blow over."

"That'd be good," I answered before leaving out the door and walking over to the schoolyard.

Passing by a group of older boys, I watched them till one called, "Darby, my mama says your daddy's a communist!"

I ignored them and went inside. In the hallway, I wondered what a communist was and if it meant his mama thought Daddy was a bad person.

*　　*　　*

That afternoon, I sat quiet in the back seat of the Chevrolet as McCall teetered through town toward home. As we went along, our friends jumped off the car fenders and running boards. Watching them, it seemed to me that they swooped away so graceful they were part turkey buzzard. It was nice, except that three of the kids who normally hang so tight to the car refused to ride with us.

That made me feel worse. I looked out a window and could feel tears scooting down my face. I didn't know how I was going to get myself and my family out of the fix I'd caused, but I wanted to. I wanted to forget all about blacks and their problems. I wanted to set up penny peeks and do pole-vaulting and play with dolls or get in my dress-up clothes. I wanted to fetch my tobacco bag of pretty marbles and play a game or jump rope to a song. Instead of worrying, climbing a springy tree would be better. I could ride it slow to the ground, like it was hooked with giant pulleys. Maybe I'd ask my mama and McCall to play croquet out front. I just wanted to have good, regular fun again. I didn't want to be a newspaper girl who was supposed to tell the truth all the time. I wanted to be a normal girl from then on.

At home, my mama was collecting the pecans that'd blown from the trees during the storm. She had Annie Jane and Aunt Greer helping her gather out back, but they weren't finding as many as a kid could. Kids are better at that sorta thing. When I changed, I went outside and said that I could ask Evette to help when she got home, and my mama didn't even bat an eye. She seemed fine about that.

"We aren't doing very well so far," Aunt Greer told me.

Mama said, "Where's McCall?"

"He left out the front door."

"Figures," she muttered. "If he was here, I'd tell him what I'm gonna tell you. If you want a Christmas present this year, you better start searching."

"That's what I'm gonna do," I told her softly, taking up a croaker sack and walking down toward the dairy barn. Before I started, I looked up at the weavy, curvy limbs of the pecan trees my granddaddy had planted, and they reminded me of swoopy, torn nets. Behind them, the crystal blue sky was so bright it almost hurt my eyes.

Scooting off to the beginning of the cotton field, I searched and searched, finding a load of pecans under every few plants. The first rows of cotton bushes had caught them like baseball mitts. On the edge of the dirt road leading back to the dairy barn, there were pecans in every mule hoof print. In the tallish grass, pecans were hidden like Easter eggs. In the woods between the dairy barn and the chicken house, pecans were underneath leaves and even stuck in the branches of small shrubs.

I'd worked for an hour by myself when I finally spotted Evette and her brothers. Dropping my sack, I tore off through a line of dried cotton bushes, their leaves crackling against my hips. By their house, I called, "Hey, guys."

As she got closer, Evette stared at me like I was a slobbering dog, like I had rabies.

"What?" I wanted to know.

Standing in front of me, seeming embarrassed, she whispered, "Everybody heard about what happened last night. Daddy said he could see the cross from our back windows."

Feeling strange, I told her, "It doesn't matter. My family isn't worried about it."

"It don't look that way on your face."

"What're you talking about?" I asked.

Softly, she said, "Your face looks sad."

A hard lump took ahold of my throat.

She corrected herself. "Your face sorta looks worried, is what I'm meaning."

"I'm not worried or sad," I lied.

She fiddled a hand in her pocket and gazed out toward the pecan trees. "What're y'all doing?"

I said, "Picking up pecans that the storm knocked from the trees. It's easy. You . . . you wanna come help?"

She said, "All right."

After Evette had changed her clothes, me and her walked toward Ellan, where Mama and Aunt Greer and Annie Jane smiled and quit, saying they were tired. Together they went inside, which was good for us. Alone, me and Evette found a ton of pecans and nearly loaded two croaker sacks full. It was fun, too. We made games out of it. First we came up with a different person's name for every pecan we found. The one who couldn't think of a new name lost. After going on and on, I got stuck after Evette said, "Kwasi," which is a name I never heard of. After that, we counted to thirty, and when we got there we checked to see who had found the most pecans. We did that over and over again. When we got bored, we decided that each time we found twenty-five pecans we had to pole-vault over a higher and higher fence till we knocked it over. Then we scratched out a hopscotch course we had to do before dropping our pecans into our sacks.

Evette said, "Let's say that when you get to the end

you gotta holler somethin' you don't like, like 'collard greens.'"

"You show me," I told her.

"All right," she said, and hopped along the squares, landing on one foot when she got to the last one. Leaning over the croaker sacks, she said, "I don't like rain."

I smiled and jumped down the course. At the end I said, "I don't like when people mess up my hair."

When she went again, she said, "I don't like dogs that bite."

On my turn, I said, "I don't like it when I wake up in the middle of the night."

We came up with about a thousand things we didn't like, and when the sun rays stretched out real far, Evette said she had to go home. A few feet into the cotton field, she stopped. Turning, she asked, "Darby, you feel better?"

I nodded. "Yeah," I said, and it was like I was turning into a baby or something. I almost cried again for liking her so much. "See you later, alligator."

Evette said, "Catch you in a while, crocodile."

*   *   *

During dinner, as we passed the greens and Daddy served up the smoked ham, Mama scolded McCall for not helping gather pecans.

He told her, "I was doing other things."

Mama balked. "Here me and Aunt Greer and Darby worked so hard to pick up pecans, and you didn't even help. You ran out the front door instead of doing work."

McCall smiled.

Mama told him, "Don't you dare look at me that way."

Because McCall was getting scolded, I smiled, too.

McCall saw me and snitched. "She's doing it now."

Mama whipped her head around. "Darby!" she said. "You wipe that smile off your face."

Apologizing, I said I would. But it wouldn't leave. Happiness was running through my arms and legs and face. Hearing Mama yell at McCall was nice. I explained to her, "My smile won't go away because it's so nice that everything seems normal."

Appreciation

On Saturday morning, so that I could go into Bennettsville early, I got up and ate breakfast with Daddy. At school the day before, like most everyone else, me and Beth had made plans to walk down to see the Gulf, which is the area where all the black-owned shops are. During the storm, most of the stores had flooded, and the owners were digging out their muddy property. We'd even heard that they had found a few dead fish in strange places, like in drawers and on shelves, and that excited us awful. After we were done there, we were going to take a picnic up to the courthouse lawn. Every Saturday farmers and their families rolled into town, and most of them rode wagons. That meant that they had to water their horses, and we liked to wait for them by the fountain. We enjoyed patting all those sweet animals.

When I woke up that morning, I felt better about everything. My arm had stopped hurting and for some reason I felt like my article was fading away, that people had stopped caring. At breakfast, I was even a little glad about things.

"Are you happy?" I asked my daddy while he ate.

Smiling, he said, "Sure. I'm happy enough." But I don't think he got what I meant. What I'd wanted to know was if he was happy right then and there, not with his life.

As I started off for Carmichael Dry Goods, the sun was skimming the very tippy-tops of trees. In the quietness of morning time, Daddy's Buick seemed like it was roaring as loud as the Bennettsville & Cheraw train. Still, the noise was all right and soothing for some reason. As we passed along, birds torpedoed off dried cotton plants, shooting away in straight lines. I'd seen it a billion times, but I always thought it was pretty. Each bird raced across the fields like they were attached to wires, getting smaller and smaller until they all the sudden disappeared. On the edge of town, a couple of crows pecked at something in the roadway, eating till we were almost on top of them. Then, in a slow manner, they flapped and jumped out of the path of our tires.

At the store, my daddy flicked on the lights and

checked his record book and pencils and fountain pens. Outside, a few folks were already waiting to get in, but he paid them no mind and did what he always does. Moving his head from side to side, he inspected the shelves to make sure nothing was in the wrong place.

When Russell arrived, my daddy checked his watch. Together, we went and sat in his office till it was exactly eight-thirty. Then he rose slowly and opened the front door. Three men came right in. I recognized two of them as brothers who worked a farm in the terrible soil up near the Sand Hills. Even though they're famous for struggling and getting nothing for it, they're real nice. Both waved to me.

The other man asked my daddy if he had a plow harness, and Daddy led him up the steps to look at the different types. Comfortable, I leaned my elbows on the counter waiting for nine o'clock, which was when I could go to Beth's house.

A lady from the Mill Village came in and went over to our selection of frying pans and pots. A few other people entered, and a man named Mr. Nathaniel signed for a sack of meal. He said, "Thank you, Little Darby," and carried it out on his shoulder.

I daydreamed about things and traced the wood-grained pattern on my daddy's store counter. I tried to count the number of circles I found, but there were so many I stopped. Then, for some reason the hairs on my neck rose like tiny cactus prickles, and I looked toward the door and saw Mr. Dunn coming through it. Right off, my heart started pounding. Twisting, I checked to see if my daddy was coming down the steps, but he wasn't.

As he approached, Mr. Dunn's lard eyes nearly sizzled and popped in his head. Towering above the counter, he said to me, "Hello, Little Darby."

Stuttering, I answered, "Ah . . . hel . . . hello, Mr. Dunn?" I heard the elevator doors close and hoped Russell was going up to fetch Daddy.

Mr. Dunn said, "I need some matches, lamp oil, and thirty feet of strong chain."

I could barely speak. "I . . . I suppose we got all that, sir. My daddy'll be down in a minute."

Mr. Dunn put a hand on the countertop. "Good. That'll give me a moment to talk with you."

Quaking, I said, "Yes . . . sir."

The lady from the Mill Village looked over.

"Now, Little Darby, let me say right off, I ain't gonna beat around the bush and treat you like a kid. Far as I'm concerned, you're an adult, or adult enough to understand my point when I get to it." Rubbing his sharp chin, Mr. Dunn said, "See, I was awfully let down with what you wrote in the paper. I was awfully bothered by what you and your black friend said about things. Top of that, to make things worse, I know your daddy helped out the Hawkins family, which was my business and not his to begin with. But I know your daddy did it. That's why I been let down with y'all," he said. "I been real let down with the way y'all are feeling so charitable toward my tenant farmers and the blacks in general."

Closing his hand, Mr. Dunn made a giant fist. "But we all make mistakes, is what I say. And I'm a Christian man, ain't I? That's why I'm gonna let it all go. I'm gonna forgive y'all, being that I know you and your family learned a proper lesson. Now, you tell me, did you learn a proper lesson from all this?"

Fingers trembling so hard I couldn't even grab up a pen, I said, "I . . . su . . . suppose, sir."

Playing like he hadn't heard me, Mr. Dunn put a hand up to one of his ears. "Didn't catch that, Little Darby. Say again?"

I couldn't talk.

"Speak up, g . . ."

My daddy cut him short. "Turpin!" he hollered, coming down the steps. "What are you doing here?"

Mr. Dunn turned and lifted his hands to play like he was innocent, reminding me of McCall. "I ain't doing nothing, Sherman. Me and your daughter was just talking."

My daddy glared at Mr. Dunn. "Turpin, your money's no good here, so I believe you ought to just go on."

Turpin laughed. "Now . . . now, I ain't doing nothing, Sherm," he said. "Far as I'm concerned, you're acting crazy. I mean, I was just making small talk with your daughter while you were busy. You tell 'im, Little Darby. Wasn't that all I was doing?"

Looking away from Mr. Dunn, I spoke up. "No . . . sir. No . . . you weren't . . . talking nice to me. You were sc . . . scaring me."

Mr. Dunn said, "Aw, Little Darby, I didn't mean ta do any such thing."

The lady from the Mill Village said, "I beg to differ with you."

My daddy snarled, "Out of my store, Turpin!" He pointed toward the door. "Now!" Daddy said.

The two farmer brothers from the Sand Hills came down the steps. "Is there a problem, Mr. Carmichael?" one of them asked.

Daddy said, "No, not as soon as Turpin leaves."

Turpin glowered at Daddy, and growled, "You throw me out, and you're gonna be sorry, Sherm. You're gonna be real sorry. Everyone from here to Columbia is gonna label you a traitor for taking the black side of things, and that's the kinda tag that'll come back to bite you, 'cause nobody likes a backstabber. Matter of fact, people are glad ta turn the other way when a backstabber gets his comeuppance."

"Leave," Daddy demanded.

"You're gonna be sor . . ."

Daddy shouted, "Leave!"

Gritting his teeth, Mr. Dunn looked about the room, looked at all of us before locking his eyes on me. He smiled.

"St . . . stop doing that," I begged, and could feel tears roll from my eyes.

Daddy bolted forward and gave Mr. Dunn a shove in the chest. "Turpin, if you want to try and intimidate somebody, you try me."

Angry, Mr. Dunn stared at Daddy like he was going to take a swipe. Balling up his fists, he leaned forward like a bull getting ready to charge. But something all the sudden changed inside of him, and he turned and yanked the front door open, tearing off a bell on a spring. "Y'all're gonna be real sorry," he declared as he left. "This ain't the end, at all."

As he passed by the front windows, someone started sobbing like they'd whacked off a finger in a cotton gin. I searched around to see who it was, but my eyes were fuzzy and blurred. Then the lady from the Mill Village wrapped her arms about me. She said, "It's okay, child. It's gonna be okay."

That's how I knew it was me making all the fuss. Feeling weak, I hugged the nice lady's dress against me.

Coming over, Daddy thanked her and politely unlatched my hands. He helped me into his office, where, sitting in his chair, I sobbed, "Mr. . . . Mr. . . . Mr. Dunn, he . . . he . . . nearly hit you, Daddy! He . . . he . . . nearly hit your face."

Daddy wrapped his arms tight about me. "Darby, honey, it's all right. He wasn't going to do any such thing."

"But . . . but . . . Daddy, all a Marlboro County's gonna hate us so . . . so bad."

"That isn't true," he whispered. "That isn't so. We're going to be fine. We're going to be all right. We've got deep roots and good friends around here."

I shook my head. "But . . . but I heard him, Daddy. I heard him say he was gonna get us for backstabbing."

"He's just talking," Daddy promised, patting my cheeks. "He's only talking."

Between tears, I hiccupped. "All right. All right, Daddy," I said, but I didn't feel like it would be all right.

"Don't pay him any mind at all. Don't," he told me.

"But . . ." I said, hiccupping, "what if he tells the Ku Klux Klan? What if —"

"Darby, nothing's going to happen."

After a minute, I sniveled. "Yes, sir."

"That's my girl," he said to me. "Be strong."

We sat that way for a while, and I told him, "I wish I wasn't crying."

"I know," he said. "I know you do. Now, come on, you wipe your eyes and I'll walk you down to the Fairchilds' house. What I want is for you to forget about this and have fun. You just let it fall from your head and have a good day. For me, all right?"

"Yes, sir," I answered, sniffling hard.

"You let it go, sweetheart."

*   *   *

Standing at the door to the Fairchilds' giant, presidential-seeming house, with the wet smell of Marlboro County filling the air, my daddy asked Beth to fetch her father. Obliging, she ran into the shadows of their home, past a chair that Jefferson Davis, who is famous for being the Southern president during the Civil War, had sat in once.

When Mr. Fairchild came to the door, my daddy said, "Robert, I'd appreciate a quick conversation. Do you mind?"

"Of course not," Mr. Fairchild answered. "Come on in."

Daddy followed me and Beth into the cool hallway. After giving me a kiss on the head, he said, "Darby, you be good."

"Yes, sir."

My daddy and Mr. Fairchild walked off toward the library.

Beth said, "What do you wanna do?"

I answered, "I don't know."

"Maybe we should go on and see the flood damage?"

Feeling uncertain about things, I mumbled, "If you want."

Beth went into the front closet to fetch her coat. "I wonder if they'll find more fish today."

"I wonder, too," I said in a halfhearted way.

"My daddy told me that somebody found a ditch eel inside their cash register, and it was still alive and squirming."

"Yuck," I replied, thinking that if I found a ditch eel, I might scream. Those things are so ugly. They look like big snakes with four of the littlest legs, and even though they aren't poisonous, they bite similar to a snapping turtle. Also, they make a whistling sound, which is sickening if you think about something as slimy as that whistling.

Hauling her hair up over her coat collar, Beth stopped and gave me a look. "Is something making you sad?"

I shrugged.

"Is something?" she wanted to know, her pretty lips all wrinkled.

Shrugging once more, I whispered, "Something happened at my daddy's store this morning." It made me shaky to remember Mr. Dunn. "Can we just go on and see if they find another ditch eel?"

Beth waited before saying, "I guess."

So together we strolled down the mossy, brick front walk and started up Main Street. Dragging along beside the yards and gardens filled with camellia bushes and shiny-leafed magnolia trees, I told Beth that I thought President Coolidge should live in her house on account of the little balcony that overlooks the front yard. "Every morning, he could come out and wave to people from up there."

Beth laughed.

I asked, "Do you ever wonder what the president gets to eat for dinner?"

"Probably only steak and pie."

"Yeah," I agreed.

At the corner of Townsend Street, Beth glanced at me and stopped. She crossed her arms. "Darby, I think you gotta say what happened this morning. I can't stand not knowing why you're sad."

I explained to her, "Daddy told me not to think about it."

"But telling me isn't like thinking about it," Beth declared. "It's true. We're best friends."

Hearing that, I smiled. To be honest, I knew talking about it *was* the same as thinking about it, but I told her anyway. I thought for a second. Then I blurted, "Mr. Dunn came into the store this morning and threatened me and Daddy. That's all."

Beth's eyes got big. "Like what kind of threat did he make?"

"He said people were gonna call us backstabbers and that we were gonna get our comeuppance."

Beth shook her head. "Ever since my daddy got a brick thrown at his window, I hate Mr. Dunn so much."

I said, "Me, too."

❋ ❋ ❋

Bennettsville's pretty stores were just getting going when Beth and me passed down Main Street. Alongside us, the rough, bumpy roadway puffed with dust. Farmers were arriving with their families in big wagons and trucks. Noises filled the air. There were clatters and rattles and engines rumbling while metal wagon wheels crunched alongside curbs. Dogs howled from apartment windows above the shops. Chains and straps jingled nice from horse harnesses. Folks called to people they hadn't seen in a week or two. Free of their mothers and fathers, farm kids wove down the sidewalks at full speed, stopping at the Candy Kitchen's windows to look in and dream.

We wandered past the courthouse and its important-seeming tower and wide lawn. Then we skittered along a road that swoops down toward Crooked Creek and the flooded Gulf.

Circling around a crowd, me and Beth slowed and stopped to stare at all the damage. We were both surprised. The area was a mess. Two buildings had fallen partway down, and a few others looked like they might do the same. The biggest shop, the grocery store, had lost its windows. A rowboat could have floated through. Out in front of the scratched and nicked doorway, there were drippy sacks of flour and sugar piled up in heaps. On the grass, next to a muddy stack of cans, there was a dead fish, but it wasn't all that neat to see.

Gawking at the clutter and all the people struggling to save things, my stomach turned, and I stopped thinking about Mr. Dunn and the farmer who'd spotted me.

Beth said, "This isn't as fun as I thought."

"Naw, it isn't."

Watching, Beth shook her head. "Where're the blacks gonna shop for food?"

"Maybe they'll open an emergency store?"

"You think they might have to shop at the A&P or Douglas and Johns?"

I said, "Nobody would let 'em."

"I bet," she agreed.

Covered from head to toe in sparkling orange mud, one of the black men glanced up in our direction. Placing a soggy box on the ground, he took off his cap and started up the road toward where we were standing. As he got closer, my stomach churned on account of thinking that he was going to yell at the crowd for spying.

Stopping a few yards away, the man took out a red, cowboy handkerchief from a back pocket. He wiped at smeary marks of clay on his face and nodded at me and Beth. "Ma'ams," he said.

It took a second, but I whispered, "Mister?"

Waving a dirty finger in my direction, but not right at me, he said, "My name's Mitchell, Miss Carmichael. You don't know me none, but I know your daddy 'cause my daddy works the Carmichael property out near Clio."

I didn't say anything.

"Anyways, for years I seen you in town with your daddy. I seen you up near the dry goods store. That's why I come up here to say hello. I know who you is and I know 'bout what you said in the *Bennettsville Times* this week. I just wanna tell ya it was a nice thing. It was, even though it won't do nothing."

Surprised, I asked, "Did you read it?"

He laughed in a loud, strong way. "Can't read a lick, but word about your story been going round. People knows what you done, and they 'preciate it. Thing about it is, most folks don't got any idea what you look like."

I nodded.

"It's true. If they did, they'd say hello, 'cause people are grateful for the effort. It's the first time I ever heard of anything like that getting writ up in any paper round here." He snickered. "Can you imagine a black man driving a Cadillac in Marlboro County? That's all right."

We stared at each other. "Where are you gonna get your groceries now?" I asked.

He raised his eyebrows. "Somewheres," he said.

"Do you own that grocery store?"

"Naw. But I know what's good for me. I know we gotta get it back on its feet." Scrubbing a hand across his rough hair, he told us, "Well, gotta get back to working." He turned away slow.

Beth called after him. "Did you find a ditch eel in the grocery building?"

Over his shoulder, he answered, "Naw, it was in the hardware store."

"Did anyone get bit?" she asked.

Twisting around, Mitchell smiled. "No one did. Thank goodness." Waving over his head, he carried himself back to the collapsing building, where he stopped and talked to people who were hauling out goods.

A Furious Fire

At the Fairchilds' house, their cook put a picnic basket together for me and Beth. Once it was arranged, we carried it up the street and toward the horse fountain in front of the courthouse. Going along the sidewalk, I was less worried about people and what they thought of my newspaper story. Mitchell had made me feel better.

Flattening a blanket on the brown grass, Beth and me took a seat and watched the crowds of dusty people wander past. A little ways behind us, some farm kids played tag. They shouted and howled happily until one of them tore the crotch from his good pants. Crying, he left to find his family, his head bowed.

Beth said, "You think Mary Pickford and Douglas Fairbanks ever argue about things?"

Not knowing much about either movie star, except that she's beautiful and he's handsome and good with swords, I thought about it for a second. "I bet they don't ever."

"Did you know they named their mansion Pickfair? It's the first part of both their names, put together."

My arms got goose-bumpy. "That's nice."

"Yeah. If I can't meet a prince on account of living in America, marrying a movie star might be an all-right thing."

"If he's famous enough."

"That's what I mean, a famous movie star."

"Maybe," I told her. I thought for a few seconds, and asked, "Have you ever heard of any famous news-paper girls?"

"Naw, I haven't ever."

"Me neither."

A horse and wagon clattered toward the fountain, and Beth and me hopped up from our blanket and met them by the stone water trough. The driver was a big man I'd seen a few times in my daddy's store. Wearing a round hat and nice clothes that seemed small on him, especially near his stomach, he yanked the reins hard to stop his horses. Smiling, his wife adjusted a thick coat around her shoulders as their three boys wrastled in the back of the wagon.

"Hello, ma'am and sir," me and Beth called. "Can we scratch your horses' noses?"

The man shrugged. "When they done drinking," he said, spitting snuff into a can.

Beth told the farm family, "They're real pretty."

The wife said, "We brush 'em a lot."

"It looks that way," I told her.

After we'd patted and patted those horses, they pulled away, and we sat back on our blanket and ate ham sandwiches and deviled eggs and biscuits with a dollop of jam. It was just past noon, and we drank lemonade and watched the Sanitary Café fill up with people while kids stood in line for the matinee at the Carolina Theater. Other families found their lunch baskets and blankets and spread a place for themselves on the cold lawn. A man with girls at the Murchison School settled his stuff alongside us, except that when he saw who I was, he moved across the yard. Mostly, though, everyone else who gathered to eat was friendly.

Me and Beth stayed there till about three o'clock in the afternoon, till we got chilly from a freezing wind that had kicked up. All together, we'd patted nearly fifty horses when, as we were getting ready to go, a family from Beth's church brought their mares to the fountain. We ran over.

The man, Mr. Waddle, shooed us both. "Hey now, I ain't interested in either a you two touching my horses."

Taken aback, Beth said, "But, Mr. Waddle, you let us pat 'em last time."

Hopping off his wagon, Mr. Waddle grabbed his mares by their harnesses and steered them to the water. "Here's the situation. I ain't gonna allow it no more. Your friend here, Miss Carmichael, she wrote a corrosive little article, and for that, I ain't gonna allow her ta do nothing. Forget it!"

Mrs. Waddle tried to shush her husband by saying, "Please, Sammy."

Mr. Waddle paid her no mind.

Once the horses were drinking, he said to me, "You gotta learn some respect, Darby Carmichael. If you don't, you gonna have all manner of trouble come your way. You and your family lost friends this week, that's fo' sure. Your daddy, he lost some business, too."

I slumped.

"You hear me talking to you? Y'understand what I'm saying?"

"Yes, sir," I mumbled, heading toward our blanket, which I imagined wrapping myself inside like I was the center part of a cigar. My thoughts flashed with pictures of Mr. Dunn scaring me that morning, and I shivered and felt like a little girl in a world of wolverines, McCall's number-one meanest animal along with sharks. Getting to the blanket, I stood over it like I was frozen. I stared down at the pattern of flowers and corn stalks, and slowly, like a door opening into a bright house, my brain got thinking. I stood there, and slowly, then faster, I got madder and madder at the likes of Mr. Waddle and Mr. Dunn. My courage, which must've been located beside my warm heart, caught a sudden, furious fire, and I spun about and was as bad-mannered as I ever was in my whole life. Fuming, I yelled, "Mr. Waddle!"

Surprised, he and his wife looked at me from where their horses drank.

Walking closer, I said, "You coulda told me you don't agree with what I wrote, but I suppose you're too mean and disrespectful to be friendly and you oughta be ashamed about that."

Shocked, Mr. Waddle stepped away from his horses. "You best shut your bratty mouth, girl, 'fore I have a talk with your father."

I said, "Mr. Waddle, I'm . . . I'm not the one being bratty. You're playing like a big baby 'cause I think different than you. That's brattiness. Not liking me for thinking different is being bratty."

Mr. Waddle stepped from around the fountain, so that I cocked my legs to run. Out of shape like he was, though, he must have figured he would never catch me. Instead, he declared, "You best straighten yourself out, girl. You best learn yourself some respect."

"You oughta," I said back.

Glaring at me, Mr. Waddle climbed onto his wagon and grabbed up the reins. Giving his horses a swat, he brought them about and pulled away, heading down Main Street.

✳   ✳   ✳

"Darby," Beth said as we walked to her home.

"Yeah?"

"You shoulda ignored Mr. Waddle."

"I know," I said.

At Beth's house, we shuffled upstairs to her room and sat for a while. I looked out her window and across Main Street. Surrounded with pretty trees, the houses looked like toys. "You wanna play with your dolls?"

From her bed, Beth said, "I suppose."

I told her, "Don't worry about Mr. Waddle. I'll say it was me who was rude and impolite."

"I don't think my daddy's gonna care."

We got out her two prettiest dolls and, troubled as we were, we made up a crummy story about them losing an ivory hair comb. We looked in Beth's garbage can and under her bed pillows and on top of her dresser. Finally we played like we found it on the floor by her baby doll crib. It was boring, but we got warm after being mostly cold all day, and at about four o'clock I told her I had to go back to my daddy's store.

"Sorry I messed things up."

"It's all right," she told me.

"I'm gonna tell your daddy it was me."

"Best friends get in trouble together," she said.

Leaving out the Fairchilds' front door, I went down their walkway and turned and nearly ran into Chester and Mercury, who were clip-clopping along the sidewalk. They stopped, and behind them, downtown Bennettsville looked pretty in the fading, melting daylight.

"Hey, Darby," Chester said, steam coming from his mouth.

"Hey, Chester."

"Where you going?"

"To my daddy's store."

Wiping at his nose, he looked down. "You want me and Mercury to carry you up there?"

Smiling, I told him, "That'd be a nice thing to do."

"Get on in."

Riding in Chester's wagon, teetering toward the Carmichael Block, I noticed how people grinned at us like I'd never caused an ounce of trouble in my whole life.

Chester cleared his throat. "Darby . . . your dress seems real clean."

"It . . . it got washed last week."

"It's bright."

I said, "Chester, your clothes are bright, too," causing his neck and ears to turn red.

Downtown, everything had slowed from the day, and whole blocks were nearly empty of people. The stores were lit up pretty inside, and a few customers talked or looked around before heading for their farms or homes. It seemed like the only busy places left were the Sanitary Café and the Candy Kitchen.

Embarrassed about Chester complimenting my dress, I didn't say any more till we got to my daddy's store. When we were there, I climbed from out of his goat cart and told him, "Thanks."

Shy, he looked at Mercury's backside. "Darby, whenever you wanna ride, you just gotta ask. Any time is okay."

"I'm gonna ride a lot," I said. Then, embarrassed again, I shoved through the door and into Carmichael Dry Goods.

Standing behind the counter, my daddy was talking to a farmer.

I waved.

Daddy waved back. Then he led the man toward a lineup of things like hammers and saws. Wandering over to the register, I leaned my back against it. Russell was gone for the day, and the elevator's doors were pushed wide open. For a few minutes, I watched my daddy talk to the farmer. Lifting my eyes, I searched across the street and looked at the People's Bank. It was real nice out, with the sky above purple and smooth. My eyes flitted across some rooftops, just catching partial sight of a fast, dark automobile as it howled by on the street. Then, like the whole world slowed down, there was a series of booms and two front windows flashed and exploded glass.

Before I even knew what was happening, shattering sounds filled my ears, and among that terrible breaking rain, a brick skittered down an aisle and stopped against one of my feet. After that, everything went quiet except for more pieces of falling glass and my daddy's breathing, which sounded almost exactly like a dog who'd run and run on a hot South Carolina day.

"Daddy?" I yelped.

The farmer shook himself, and glass fell from his shoulders. "You . . . you think we had an earthquake?"

Breathing hard, Daddy told him, "I don't think so."

Then he asked me, "Darby . . . Darby, sweetheart, are you okay?"

Barely able to talk, I answered weakly, "I . . . guess." I looked down at the cracked brick by the toe of my shoes and saw three big letters scraped into the top and sides. "KKK," it read. Even though it was battered and chipped, I could see it as clear as day.

Bleeding from an arm, my daddy came over to me. "Darby, sweetie?"

Scared and holding a hand over my mouth, I pointed at the brick on the floor.

Meanwhile, the farmer stumbled down the aisle and sat on a spool of wire. "Lord," he mumbled, shaking pieces of glass from his hair.

Outside, people hovered and peered in through the broken windows. What remained of the crowds along Main Street formed a half circle in front of my daddy's store. More folks came out of the Candy Kitchen, the Sanitary Café, and even the Carolina Theater. Shop-keepers left their places and rushed over. Within five minutes, word had spread into nearby homes. Shortly, the group of kids who'd been watching people dig out the Gulf rushed up the hill to gawk. Behind them, moving carefully, were several black men.

Holding his injured arm, my daddy picked up one of the bricks and went to a broken window. With a shaky voice, he asked, "Did anyone see who it was? Did anyone see anything at all?"

People shook their heads. A man shouted, "It was a gray car. That's all I noticed."

Dropping his chin, Daddy stared down at the glass shards around his feet. His jaw grew tight and clenched, and, lifting his head, he yelled, "You know what? You know why this happened?"

No one said anything, but they all knew. I could tell.

"It's because of race," my daddy declared, holding up the brick so that people could read what it said. "It's about blacks and whites and what people believe. That's why this happened." He paused before saying more. "To think that my daughter and a customer were in here when these bricks were thrown, and both could have been injured or killed because the Klan doesn't agree with an article in the paper. To me, that's just unacceptable. That's cowardly."

Not very many people seemed to agree.

Shook up and shivery, I shuffled down an aisle and, cracking hunks of glass beneath my feet, climbed onto the ledge of a shattered window. From there, I looked out at the crowd.

Daddy said, "The Klan's trying to prevent free speech about an issue we all know we're going to have to address. We all know we've gotta talk about it."

Somebody yelled, "You got sharecroppers all over your farm, Sherm, and you're saying this stuff?"

"I am, yeah," Daddy called back. "And I do have tenant farmers. I'm no saint. But I've begun to see something over the last few weeks. I understand the situation a little better, and I know things have got to give. Nobody should live fearful or hungry, not when we can do something about it. We've got to allow folks a chance to make a life in Marlboro County. As it is, blacks don't have any hope of doing that. I'm arguing that it's our job as human beings to be decent and humane and see that they get some."

"You wanna give 'em too much," somebody hollered back.

"You're wrong," my daddy called back. "No matter what you think . . ." he said, and all the sudden his voice trailed off.

That's when my eyes caught on Turpin Dunn, who was a few inches taller than the other tallest person in the crowd. He was talking to the Klan man and some other people. Seeing them I turned and called out for Daddy's attention, but he had already passed through the busted window. He was going right after them.

Mr. Dunn rose up, and shouted, "Come on! Come take your whipping, Sherman!"

Somebody shoved at Mr. Dunn's crowd. They

shoved back, causing everyone to start jostling angrily. Then, his shirt untucked and half unbuttoned, Sheriff McDonnell rushed around the corner and plunged into the crowd.

Right in front of me, it seemed like the entire town was ready to break into a horrible, giant fight. It seemed like, because of my article, somebody might get killed. Scared and guilty, I started screaming. I screamed as loud and strong as I could, over and over. "Stop it! Just stop it!" I shrieked.

It took a minute or so, but a number of people glanced my way. Seeing them, I kept on yelling, so that the rest of the mob eventually looked over, too, including my daddy and Mr. Dunn. Then, surprised I'd gotten everyone's attention, I wondered what I was going to tell them. For a short time, I tried to think of things, but my brain wasn't working like normal. So instead of thinking, I let words come from my mouth. "Don't . . . don't you know it isn't good to fight? Don't you know it doesn't make sense? We oughta treat everyone nice. That's all I was saying in my newspaper story, that we gotta be considerate. And that isn't something to fight about."

As simple as I was talking, nobody seemed to understand what I meant. People just stared at me, shocked-looking because I'd shrieked so crazy. So I kept going. "I . . . I got a best friend named Evette who's black, and you wanna know what? Me and her are the same except for she's poorer. That's what I believe. That's all. I didn't even mean to cause trouble."

Swallowing, I tried to come up with more to talk about, but it was hard. It was hard to think. "Just a few nights ago, I had a dream that all the black tenant farmers in Marlboro County floated off to New York, where they can own houses and cars and be with people who like 'em. And when they were gone, nothing grew in the cotton fields 'cause nobody was around to work. See? You gotta know we need to get along. You gotta know that."

Stopping, I stared blankly out at all our friends and neighbors. Nobody spoke for a little while. Swaying, I tried to look into every face, but there were too many.

A man told me, "You don't understand the history."

Somebody answered back, "Yeah, but it don't matter."

Another person yelled, "We need to put this arguing to rest. It don't help a difficult situation."

A weak cheer rose up.

A man near the smashed windows declared, "Listen here. I believe I'm speaking for everybody when I say we aren't gonna tolerate the Klan in Marlboro County anymore. No matter! We don't need that sort of anger on top of everything else."

"Here, here!" somebody called in agreement.

"Here, here!" a good number of people answered back.

Turpin Dunn didn't say a word.

Waving his hands over his head, Sheriff McDonnell got people to clear the way.

He glared at the Klan man. "I got something to say to you boys, so y'all listen up good. You come in here trying to cause any more trouble, and I'm gonna thump you good. Y'all'll be walking outa here in nothing but your birthday suits, or you'll be rotting in jail. I ain't kidding. Y'all just come on back and try me."

Everyone had something to say, and the crowd got loud and excited, but the fight and fury was out of them. Tired and dizzy, I felt like all the angriness had been sucked out of my body, too. Turning, I crunched down the glassy aisle, passing by the farmer who my daddy had been helping. He said something to me, but I don't know what. Like a ghost, I floated back to the Carmichael Dry Goods office, where I sat at Daddy's desk, wishing I had that little statuette of the horse and Robert E. Lee. I wished I could play and get my mind off what had happened, because my head was so full it felt empty.

As Pretty as Heaven

Since last fall, what I've learned about things is that people don't change fast or easy and sometimes not at all. Still, after my daddy's windows were broken out, I feel like all of Marlboro County's been trying to be more thoughtful. Every week there are meetings held at Mr. and Mrs. Fairchild's house, where everyone from tenant farmers to shopkeepers discuss the things that need changing. That's when people decided to open the A&P and Douglas and Johns to blacks. Considering the way things were, that was big. And even though people were nervous, the Ku Klux Klan didn't burn crosses or smash windows or anything. It's like they've been scrubbed out around here. Mean Mr. Dunn has stayed quiet out on his farm. As a matter of fact, he hasn't made a peep in months.

My daddy and Mr. and Mrs. Fairchild are pushing for better black schools and new books and buildings, but there isn't much money to go around, so nothing will change for a while. I asked Daddy why blacks can't go to the Murchison School, and he said it might happen one day, but that type of change takes a long time.

Still, I wish Evette was in class with me and Beth. Me and her and Beth would be like sisters, telling secrets and stories and passing notes. Unless Miss Burstin caught us a lot, we might pass a thousand notes a year.

At the start of the winter, around Christmastime, Evette and I started writing for the *Bennettsville Times* again. We like writing so much, is why. Sometimes we try to make people see the truth about important things, but we haven't done anything else about blacks and whites.

In February, Mr. Salter began paying us fifty cents a column. He also told me to write an article about everything that happened between my daddy and Mr. Dunn and the Ku Klux Klan. I didn't exactly want to, but I tried. The thing is, my story kept getting bigger and bigger so that it wouldn't fit in the newspaper, till it turned into a small book. Mr. Salter didn't mind. He helped me and Evette edit so that it makes better sense, which is good because I know it was a little bumpy. I know it seemed like the only reason I was writing was because I don't like Mr. Dunn so much, and Mr. Salter fixed that.

But, the truth is, I still don't like Mr. Dunn. I don't, even though I'm trying to forgive him. As a matter of fact, just yesterday McCall made a list of the meanest men who ever lived, and he said that Mr. Dunn was number twenty, after Kaiser Wilhelm, who was the boss of Germany during the war in Europe. That made sense to me. The thing is, McCall's number-one meanest is Genghis Khan, who a long time ago captured all of China. He said that Mr. Khan would cut Mr. Dunn's head clean off without even thinking about it. That's why Mr. Dunn was way down at number twenty. In fact, McCall said, sticking Mr. Dunn on his list was just a big joke. He laughed at me about it, but I didn't think it was funny. I think that's exactly where Mr. Dunn belongs, on the twenty-meanest-men-who-ever-lived list.

Since last fall, my mama's changed. Since the night the Ku Klux Klan burned that cross on our property, she's been trying to think differently. During the winter, she explained to me that she had a lifetime of habit behind her feelings, and that it's hard to shake that stuff loose. Sometimes she can't do it. In spite of that, she started a class to teach blacks who never learned how to read. Also, she's a lot nicer about Evette. As a matter of fact, Evette's been over to dinner a few times since the fall, and just last week, Mama let her spend the night with me and Beth. Early in the afternoon, when the three of us got back from our schools, we ran through the new-planted cotton fields to go swinging in the woods. When we were done, we rushed back to Ellan and rode bikes around in the backyard. Evette borrowed McCall's while me and Beth rode our own. In the patchy dust beside the smokehouse, Evette constantly fell over. Being real nimble, she never did get hurt and always came up laughing. We all laughed. We laughed so hard we got bellyaches.

"How . . . how come you can't ride a bike?" Beth finally snorted.

"'Cause I only done it twice before," Evette explained, smiling.

I pedaled around fast and furious, with King chasing after me, barking and leaping. I skidded sideways in front of the Grab and put my foot down. Standing there, looking back at my friends, who I love, and Ellan, which I also love, I could see the whole big South Carolina sky over their heads and above the outbuildings and the pecan trees, and it had to be as pretty as Heaven. I promise. And noticing it got me sad for people like Great-Uncle Harvey, who's so nice but still blind. I would hate not to be able to see the flat ground rushing away from my feet, rubbing the sky. I would hate not to see Marlboro County, South Carolina, with nearly everything perfect about it except for a few important things that can change. And those important things are changing, too. Miss Burstin and my daddy say so to me a lot. As a matter of fact, just three days ago McCall was carrying us home from school when a black man drove by in an old, beat-up truck. The man's face was happy, and one of his hands was relaxed and out the window. And even though it wasn't hardly a fancy car, it wasn't a Cadillac, I saw a black man driving. Right then and there, it seemed to me that as pretty as Marlboro County is, it's only gonna get prettier, and that's the truth.

Author's Note

The characters in *Darby* are loosely based on a series of oral history interviews that I've been conducting in Marlboro County, South Carolina, since 1997.

Conceived by my good friend Catherine G. Rogers, who grew up just outside of Bennettsville, The Marlboro Narrative Project is an attempt to record smaller, contextual aspects of the area's history before the people who remember them are gone. In the beginning, Catherine and I sought to document myths, historical details, and even lost sayings. However, in our hours spent in the company of retired farmers and housemaids, politicians and day laborers, we have learned so much more. The project remains a labor of love for both of us.

Two years ago, while driving south for another week of interviews, I began to imagine Darby's story. While discussing the work ahead, I asked Catherine whether she'd mind if I tried to weave our interviews into a novel.

It seemed natural. The people we'd spoken with painted such vivid, beautiful, and alien pictures that there was an absolute need to present them to a generation that hasn't heard — or maybe hasn't heard enough — about the everyday struggles and triumphs of the past. As usual, Catherine was an enthusiastic supporter.

The participants in The Marlboro County Narrative Project were big-hearted men and women who were at once excited and worried about our mission. Some were concerned that we would misrepresent the times and the people who lived them. Nevertheless, most everyone put aside their fears and opened their lives to us. Their cooperation and goodwill allowed me to create Darby's story. In light of that, I need to thank the following individuals for their generosity: Harriet Charles Fairfield, Helen Breeden, Charles F. Hollis, Sr., William L. Kinney, Jr., Hampton and Lucy MacIntyre, Hubbard McDonald, T. A. O'Neal, Jr., Jennings Owens, Jr., Eula K. Prince, Catherine M. Rogers, Frank B. Rogers, Jr., Bright Stubbs, and William Weatherly. If I left someone out, please forgive the oversight. Those interviews can be heard at the Marlboro County Historical Society in Bennettsville, South Carolina.

Darby is a fictitious character. Certainly, many aspects of her life and the lives of people in the book are based on recollections and history, but her love for writing and the troubles it generates are my own invention. Also, I chose not to employ the words "colored" or "Negro," even though they were commonly used in 1926. These days, both are considered offensive, and I did not want to perpetuate derogatory language for young readers.

Finally, I want to thank my beautiful wife and daughter, both of whom are patient and inspiring whenever I attempt to write. I'd also like to express gratitude to my hardworking and loyal agent, Robbie Hare; to my wonderful editor at Candlewick Press, Liz Bicknell; and to Deborah Wayshak, her fantastic and helpful associate. I hope that *Darby* makes everyone involved proud.

Jonathon Scott Fuqua
February 2002

THE REAPPEARANCE OF
SAM WEBBER

Jonathon Scott Fuqua

"A white eleven-year-old becomes fast friends with a black janitor and learns about racism, loss, grief, forgiveness, and the landscape of Baltimore in this heartfelt ... debut." *Publishers Weekly*

"Addresses prejudice and overcoming urban fears ... a realistic picture of the trials in a single-parent family... Highly recommended." *Library Journal*

A *Teen People* Book Club Selection

Winner of the ALA 2000 Alex Award

A *Booklist* Editors' Choice

A New York Public Library Book for the Teen Age

An American Booksellers Foundation for Free Expression List Choice

A *School Library Journal* Best Book of the Year

DOVEY COE
Frances O'Roark Dowell

"My name is Dovey Coe and I reckon it don't matter if you like me or not. I'm here to lay the record straight, to let you know them folks saying I done a terrible thing are liars. I aim to prove it, too. I hated Parnell Caraway as much as the next person, but I didn't kill him."

Dovey Coe likes to speak her mind. She tells her beautiful older sister Caroline just what she thinks about no-good rich boy Parnell Caraway hanging round their house all summer. And she's quick to speak up for her deaf brother Amos when folks treat him like he's slow. But sometimes, speaking your mind can get you in a whole lot of trouble – as Dovey Coe discovers. Accused of murder, who will speak up for *her*?

Winner of the Mystery Writers of America's Edgar Award

BECAUSE OF WINN-DIXIE
Kate DiCamillo

One summer's day, ten-year-old India Opal Buloni goes down to the local supermarket for some groceries – and comes home with a dog.

Winn-Dixie is no ordinary dog. Big, skinny and smelly he may be, but he also has the most winning smile. It's because of Winn-Dixie that Opal gets to know some very surprising people and starts to make new friends. It's because of Winn-Dixie that she finally dares to ask her father about her mother, who left when Opal was three. In fact, just about everything that happens that summer is because of Winn-Dixie.

Read about the exploits of this most unusual dog and a host of quirky characters in this enchanting tale.

A Newbery Honor Book